'This thoroughly delightful n
narrator tells Harvey's fictiona
dry, sly wit. Humour is added as deftly as a cordon-bleu chef might flavour a dish . . . A comic masterpiece' *Daily Telegraph*

'This high comedy, which I thoroughly recommend, has a darker theme than some of Teresa Waugh's earlier books. She is one of the most distinctive, abrasive comedians on the literary scene' *Daily Mail*

'Waugh specialises in the self-deceptions that arise as people squirm away from themselves, dodging their uncomfortable memories. In *A Friend Like Harvey* she produces a beguilingly credible monster to portray this theme. [An] elegantly contrapuntal study of two different versions of self-deceit. As modest and self-effacing as its narrator, this is a small, still and austerely realistic depiction of how we go about failing to remember each other' *Spectator*

'An acid-sharp portrait of a lovable cad. A beautifully controlled, witty and absorbing comedy of manners'

Good Housekeeping

'In this wry, quietly subversive novel, Teresa Waugh delineates a very English kind of monster. She has always been adept at peeling away the polite surface of the contemporary scene among the middle and upper classes . . . Now she turns her cool and unforgiving eye on a certain type of Englishman, the sort who used to be known as a fearful bounder or a terrible cad. As she shows with understated skill, such amiable Wodehousean labels, which convey as much affection as disapproval, often disguise something much nastier and more dangerous . . . A cleverly constructed and well-observed morality tale'

Anne Chisholm

Teresa Waugh has translated numerous books from French and Italian. Her previous novels include *Song at Twilight, Sylvia's Lot* and *The Gossips*. She lives in Somerset.

A Friend Like Harvey

TERESA WAUGH

PHŒNIX

A PHOENIX PAPERBACK

First published in Great Britain by Victor Gollancz in 1999
This paperback edition published in 2000 by Phoenix,
an imprint of Orion Books Ltd,
Orion House, 5 Upper St Martin's Lane,
London WC2H 9EA

A CIP catalogue record for this book
is available from the British Library.

ISBN 0 75381 044 1

Printed and bound in Great Britain by
The Guernsey Press Co. Ltd, Guernsey, C.I.

Part I

Chapter I

Harvey is a tall man, lean – perhaps spare would be a better word – and dark. Well, I suppose he's grey now but I can't help thinking of him as dark. He always was dark – very dark, with dark rings under his eyes and a five-o'clock shadow by early afternoon. The sort of man who needs to shave twice a day. Harvey is not nearly as good-looking as he would like to think he is but somehow his apparent confidence in his power to attract the opposite sex can dazzle people – women at least – so that they have overlooked – in the past anyway – the fact that a short nose and long upper lip lend his face a strangely childish, expectant look and that his large ears protrude a little.

Harvey likes women. He always has done and has never hesitated to boast of his conquests. It has occasionally crossed my mind that some of the conquests of which he boasts may have taken place in the realm of fantasy only.

For instance years ago there was Lucinda. It seems particularly unlikely that anyone of Lucinda's calibre could even have looked at Harvey. I remember her as a serious, careful person who never, it seems, does anything at all rash. And there have been countless others, real or imaginary, I'll never know.

Harvey takes life as it comes, allows it to wash over him, buffet him this way and that and somehow, like the proverbial reed, he bends and sways but never snaps. He laughs off his misfortunes and is apparently unscathed by them; he even turns them to his own advantage, twists events to put himself in a more favourable light, to show himself perhaps as a likeable buffoon, someone who is too easy-going to bother, everybody's friend, a man who never thought it worth while going into battle. Life's-too-short sort of thing. Yet life for him has been full of disappointments. I can't count the number of times he's told me exactly why it was that he never made the Surrey cricket eleven all those years ago.

At his public school Harvey was an outstanding cricketer, with a brilliant future in store, but a long series of misfortunes, misunderstandings and injustices deprived him of the glory he so richly deserved and, according to him, deprived Surrey not only of a fine medium-pace bowler, but also of a man with the ability to score runs when they were most needed. But of course it had been all to the good in the end. At Cambridge there'd been no time to concentrate on cricket, what with one thing and another. It certainly wasn't work which interfered, as I seem to remember Harvey coming down with a very mediocre degree. Anyway, it would never have suited Harvey to have taken up cricket seriously, he would have missed out on so many other things – women and so forth. All those hours in the nets and the discipline – the confounded discipline. Harvey has always liked to boast about how he flouts discipline, takes his own line, does his own thing. But you can usually sense a vein of bitter-sweet nostalgia whenever he returns to the theme of what might have been, and, because Harvey is quite lovable, you feel sorry for him and almost get a lump in the throat. That is until you've heard the same song sung once too often.

Singing – now there's something else that Harvey's rather good at. He loves it and has always reminded me of Keats's nightingale, singing of summer with full-throated ease. He used to go to church – I doubt he does still – in order, I supposed, to belt out all those hymns, drowning the tremulous sopranos of the few old ladies in the congregation with his own mellifluous baritone. 'For all the Saints' and 'Onward Christian Soldiers', those were his favourites. But he also loves opera and his house has frequently echoed to him singing the best-known arias of Puccini, Mozart or Donizetti.

Harvey has never learned to play a musical instrument, although he will tell you that he has always regretted not playing the piano. He would have loved to play the piano and he'll explain at length why exactly he was never able to take it up. Talk, talk, talk – that's Harvey for you. Too old now of course to take up anything new, but then, in days gone by, when he was young and could have done it easily, he could never find the time.

Harvey is well off – or was. As a boy he inherited a certain amount of money from a bachelor great-uncle somewhere in the north. The money was well invested and well looked after so that by the time he grew up there was a nice little fortune waiting for him. Shortly after he married – very young that first time – he was able to buy an elegant Queen Anne house and a small farm in one of the Home Counties. He had thought of going to the West Country but it was too far away and perhaps he thought that farming there might be more like the real thing. In those days he dabbled in farming and could talk of nothing but breeds of cattle, milk production, cattle disease and so forth. Most of his friends were quite glad when he moved on from this particular passion although it was rather sad in some ways because it coincided with his moving on from his marriage and everybody felt sorry for Deirdre. She was bereft by the break-up, whereas Harvey appeared to have extricated himself unscathed from the experience.

When Harvey came down from Cambridge he was, because of his inheritance, considerably better off than the rest of us and although he paid lip-service to the idea of getting himself a job, he never seemed to make any great effort in that direction. He certainly didn't have any idea of what he wanted to do whilst being quite adamant about all the things he wouldn't dream of doing. His father urged him towards accountancy, which he deemed boring and too much like hard work. The City he considered boring, too, and he certainly had no vocational aptitude for any of the professions. 'Imagine being a doctor,' he would say. 'You spend seven years studying how to spend the rest of your life sticking your finger up people's backsides.'

The law again was too much like hard work and anyway, Harvey had an idea that lawyers were odious people. So after a summer spent running around Europe in an Austin Seven with someone called Geoffrey who was his sidekick at the time, instead of looking for gainful employment, Harvey set about looking for a wife.

Deirdre was a small pale girl and at the time it was rather surprising that Harvey should have spared her a second glance. She was only eighteen when they became engaged and had just finished a secretarial course. Harvey dragged her around London showing her off to his friends, who sniggered unkindly behind her back while she timorously simpered, proud, we imagined, of her eligible catch. The wedding was to be in St Peter's, Eaton Square, and we were all invited. The first of our friends to marry.

Deirdre is the youngest of three daughters. Both her older sisters waited until their mid-twenties to marry, which in those days was late, so when she announced her intention, at such a tender age, of plighting her troth to rich young Harvey Hotham, her parents were delighted. They felt that when this wedding was over they could heave a great sigh of relief, consider their life's work accomplished, leave London and retire to a quiet rural existence in Lincolnshire whence they came. With this in mind they happily pushed the boat out and floated their poor innocent lamb on the high seas. She, with no idea how to put her hand to the tiller and with her mousy hair pinned back in what used to be called a French pleat.

How well I remember that wedding, which must have been in '57 or '58. Geoffrey was best man, of course, and he and Harvey were at the church well in time, Harvey looking as jaunty as ever – thoroughly pleased with himself, in fact, turning and nodding and waving at his friends as they took their places in the pews.

When Deirdre arrived with her father, I remember feeling, as she shimmered down the aisle to strains of Handel, her face hidden behind a white veil, that she looked more like a ghost than a human being. Some kind of ethereal revenant from a past age. She appeared to have no substance. Her vows were unable to be heard at the back of the church whereas Harvey's 'till death us do part' echoed loud and clear and confident. What did he think he was doing?

As she came back down the aisle with her veil thrown back, the married woman already seemed to have gained some substance. They'd put a lot of make-up on her, and her mother's pearl choker, and she smiled prettily like the girl who has won the beauty contest. Still she was timorous, like a young hind scenting the spring air.

I wasn't sure where they were going for their honeymoon after we waved them off from the Hyde Park Hotel, she in a huge pink flowery hat, but I do remember hearing that, due to some incompetence of Harvey's, who'd left the tickets behind, they missed the plane that night and had to slink back through a side door and weren't in fact able to leave until the next morning.

Only recently Deirdre reminded me that they'd been to Venice. It is easy to imagine Deirdre trudging around Venice in those dreadful stiletto heels that were the fashion, twisting her ankle on steps over bridges, clasping a guidebook in her hands, quite unprepared for what she was looking at, knowing nothing of Palladio or Tintoretto, oblivious to the beauty because of her struggle to understand it and her struggle to please Harvey. Dismayed perhaps by Harvey's insouciance. Distressed by his inability to understand her – to enter her soul. Unsure of herself, unable to make love, miserable. Who knows?

Deirdre told me years later that on looking back she could see that things had been wrong from the start.

Harvey, I imagine, would have wanted to spend his time in Harry's Bar or Cipriani's or some other smart venue. He would have wanted to sit in Florian's on the Piazza San Marco and to stretch his legs to the sound of cheap music as he read a two-day-old copy of the *Daily Mail* and vaguely watched pigeons and the world go by – watched the pretty Italian girls. He would have been bored, not really knowing what to do, while Deirdre did her best to learn and to appear intelligent for his sake. I suppose he must have taken her in a gondola.

Harvey, of course, had done his national service in Cyprus and had already been to Italy with Geoffrey that summer when they came down from Cambridge, so he felt very much at ease – in any case Harvey generally affects to feel at ease with his endless chatter, which I've always supposed hides a nervous disposition, a butterfly mind and a deep sense of insecurity. But he had certainly been better educated than Deirdre and was far more sophisticated, so he would have dazzled her with his Carpaccios and his Crivellis. He would also have had introductions to one or two Venetian *nobili signori* and surely must have stridden off to visit them, Deirdre trailing painfully behind in those frightful shoes, her feet swelling in the unaccustomed heat.

Deirdre, who had never been abroad before, would have sat nervously on the edge of her gilt chair not knowing what to make of the glass of Carpano she clutched in a muggy paw. Harvey, on the other hand, would have been quite expansive, throwing out his arms as he dropped the names of his parents' smarter friends, most of whom, if they thought about him at all, would have forgotten that he was no longer a child.

'Do you know So-and-So?' I hear the Venetian noblemen ask, dropping the name of some well-known personage. And I hear Harvey lying in reply. Deirdre sitting there amazed by the big, wide world and the sophistication of her man.

It is impossible to think quite why Harvey married Deirdre in the first place. He never appeared to like her very much, certainly he never seemed in the least bit interested in her and was never – in public at any rate – particularly nice to her. We all felt sorry for her, especially because she, in gratitude perhaps for his having noticed her, evidently idolized him, quoting his opinion on every subject and praising his real or imagined talents at every opportunity. He must, one presumes, have been attracted to her but it seems that what attraction there was wore thin quite soon. She had a little money of her own, came from a respectable county family, but above all she was nice, in a quiet sort of way, yet there were plenty of other girls around who might have suited Harvey better and who would have been better able to stand up to the know-all, overweening manner he adopted in those days with women. Those others had a lucky escape. For poor Deirdre the marriage could only have been a painful and humiliating disaster – a disaster from which she certainly took some time to recover, for it was a while before she emerged in her true colours.

For the first year or two of their marriage, Harvey and Deirdre lived in a terraced house in Chelsea, somewhere off the King's Road. Harvey complained a good deal about the expense of running it and talked idly about looking for a job but could never find one to suit him. He spent a considerable amount of time lunching with friends in the City and discussing his future and he spent a certain amount of time in salerooms buying clumsy paintings to cover the somewhat bare walls of his house. Most weekends he and Deirdre spent out of London.

What Deirdre did in those days, I truly don't know. What did any young married woman without children and without a job do? Perhaps she shopped in Peter Jones, met friends of her own for lunch and gave dinner parties. It is hardly surprising if she fell victim to depression.

In any case the move to the country seemed initially to revivify the pair of them. A change in the air, a new house to decorate and Harvey, from the depths of his ignorance, banging on about shorthorns and Friesians and artificial insemination. He really fancied himself as a farmer for a while.

Harvey has always been a man with the ability to see himself from the outside suddenly as a certain type of person and then to force himself, however awkwardly and unsuitably, into that role. I well remember, some years later, staying with friends who received an unexpected call from Harvey, who was at the local railway station. He'd made some muddle over the trains, got out at the wrong station and so missed a connection or something. Anyway, he was on his way back from a fishing holiday. Fishing? Harvey? He came to stay the night, and I fetched him from the station. I found him in the waiting room, most uncharacteristically dressed in a flat cap, in sludge green from head to foot and carrying waders and a fishing rod. He was overplaying the part, standing there, holiday over, still dressed for the salmon reaches, with his lower lip thrust out, mouth down at the corners, looking, as he supposed, for all the world like a really serious sportsman. He was between marriages then and busy, I suppose, trying to impress some smart angling girl.

It was just the same when Harvey was being a farmer. He strode around the place in wellington boots, his thumb stuck into the fork of a gnarled stick. Sometimes he tied binder twine round his waist and leaned on a gate chewing grass, and he wore big what used to be called 'fisherman-knit' pullovers with holes in the elbows, which he affected not to notice, although I sometimes thought he put them there on purpose. Harvey, who until then had always been something of a dandy who sneered at his brother farming in Scotland and who certainly, even now, pays a great deal of attention to what he wears. Very careful to dress young – but not too young – always to be correctly dressed for the occasion, never to wear brown shoes with a blue suit and so forth.

Everyone expected Deirdre to start having babies once she'd moved to the country, but she didn't; instead she acquired a Cairn terrier on which she doted fiercely. It was allowed everywhere – on the bed, on the sofas, in the bed – which really was strange considering how overdecorated the house was.

Deirdre obviously enjoyed doing the house up, especially as there seemed to be plenty of money to throw around. The whole place was a swirl of wallpapers and chintzes and thick-pile carpets and swags and bows and matching this and matching that and blue roses and pink birds and ivy climbing up trellises – all quite at odds with the new farmer that was Harvey. Now all these years later it's extraordinary to think of Deirdre in those surroundings.

Only recently she said something about the dreadful taste we all had years ago. 'It makes me quite claustrophobic to think about Shackles now,' she remarked. 'So over done up!'

Shackles – that was the name of the house. Funny name. Pretty house. It was a Queen Anne red brick house with a fine oak staircase rising out of the back halls with long, low rooms on either side of the hall and a delicate Adam-style marble mantelpiece in the drawing room. I remember that Harvey and Deirdre were both very pleased with that fireplace. You never went to Shackles but one of them commented on it, remarked on how it simply 'made' the room. They'd put a club fender in front of it, which to my mind was somewhat out of place.

To the right of the house as you came up the drive was a yard enclosed on two sides by some grand old barns with deep, sloping tiled roofs. The garden round the house was well tended and delightfully old-fashioned with hornbeam and yew hedges and a wide lawn dominated by a copper beech and a splendid cedar tree. There was a vegetable garden hidden somewhere behind the hedges and beyond the lawn were gently undulating fields and then a church tower surrounded by the clustered roofs of the village, all half concealed by the brow of the hill.

Everyone loved weekends at Shackles. When there were large numbers, Deirdre used to hire a weekend cook who provided elaborately rich food which we thought was wonderful, and there was always plenty to drink, and we all showed off and shouted a good deal. In summer Harvey played cricket with the village team. We played badminton or croquet and backgammon, and some people played bridge whilst Deirdre tried to keep a semblance of order, because although the Cairn terrier was allowed to do just what it liked, we were not supposed to wreck the place with muddy boots and spilt drinks, rings on the furniture and so forth.

The first time Frances and George stayed must have been in June or July because I remember eating gooseberry fool out on the lawn at lunchtime and Frances looking up to say something with the light shining on her face so that I couldn't help noticing that her eyes were green – almost the colour of gooseberries.

Frances and George were the flavour of the month. Frances was somebody's sister – a little older than the rest of us – and George was older still. They'd been married for five or six years at the time and had just come back from a stint abroad, suddenly to become everyone's new best friends. The sixties had hardly begun, so Frances was a little before her times, talking about free love and mind-enhancing drugs until we were all quite dazzled. She was beautiful, too, and that helped. George was very cool, long and lank as Harvey, but indolent almost to the point of inertia. It was hard to imagine him working in a bank, which was apparently exactly what he did, earning an exorbitant amount of money. Frances and George were golden people, or so it seemed at the time. Besides, we were all very young, so we were delighted to have these new, older friends who flattered us by their very presence.

I think it was on that particular weekend that Harvey decided to drop the farmer disguise – or perhaps he had been preparing for the transformation for a little while. He appeared for dinner on Saturday evening dressed in a mauve shirt with a narrow tie covered in little forget-me-nots. Gone was the fisherman-knit, gone the rugged farmer's grimace; lower jaw thrust forward, mouth grimly down at the corners. Here was a new, debonair Harvey. With what in mind, one wondered.

Deirdre, it suddenly dawned on me, although still quiet and withdrawn, had gradually changed over the last few years. Perhaps she had gained in confidence, proud of her lavish, comfortable home and the hospitality it dispensed, pleased that we all flocked there for weekends. She also seemed relieved to think that Harvey might have found his *métier* and so encouraged him to put as much binder twine as he liked round his waist. She had cut her hair, no longer wearing it in a tight little chignon; somehow she seemed altogether more relaxed, at ease in her home, more ready to laugh, less tense about everything having to be just so. Yet, caught in repose as she sat by the marble fireplace with her dog on her lap, her face betrayed a faraway melancholy. Between her and Harvey there never seemed to be any communication beyond whatever might be needed on a domestic level, and to the rest of us she remained somewhat distant – almost as if she were set apart, not one of the gang, merely its agreeable hostess and provider. It was impossible to guess what she really felt or thought.

At dinner there was Harvey in his mauve shirt and floral tie, talking away, holding the floor as usual. Talk, talk, talk. As his chatter became more outlandish, a tendency to stammer became more noticeable. The price of cattle feed, he told us, was becoming exorbitant so that dairy farming was soon going to be a thing of the past in this country. We all oohed and aahed at the tragedy of no longer seeing our English meadows grazed by long-faced Guernseys and soft-eyed Jerseys. Luckily no one had heard of mad cows in those days, or God knows what yarn Harvey would have spun.

On and on he went, talking about molasses and cow cake and this and that. Did we realize, he wanted to know, that it took so many hundreds of tons of raw cane sugar to produce one tablespoonful of molasses, which in itself was pure, unsaturated alcohol such as was used in making rum, Indian toddy and arrack, which meant that the average daily alcohol intake of a G-Guernsey cow during the winter months was exactly such and such a percentage of its entire nourishment. The Molasses Act of 1733 had been designed to protect the West Indian sugar trade but had resulted only in farmers being ruined nearly two hundred years later, and in severe alcohol poisoning among cattle. Harvey could assure us that with his very own eyes, he had seen a herd of Friesian cows in Germany, 40 per cent of which was suffering from DTs. And if we didn't believe him, he could refer us to an Italian count of his acquaintance who had not only witnessed the same thing, but who had seen a hundred intoxicated sheep – egregious in their drunkenness – each one leaving the flock to wander alone, all because they had been eating the p-p-pips and husks of grapes intended for the production of grappa.

That's Harvey for you. Once he's in full flow, there's no stopping the jumble of fact and fiction that pours from his lips – and we were hanging upon every word, all of us laughing as we imagined the inebriated Friesians lurching across the plains of Lower Saxony. Only Frances proceeded to eat her tournedos Rossini with a straight face. It could have been that she thought Harvey a little childish, or then, it could have been that she, so beautiful and in a way so superior, demanded attention which she was not getting.

In order to feel real, Frances always needed to see her reality reflected in the eyes of those around her. Frances needed – for all I know still needs – admiration in order to survive and although she most particularly enjoyed the admiration of men, she also needed her ego to be bolstered by women, who must of necessity be less pretty and less vivacious than she. She had a kind of power not only over men but over some women as well, one or two of whom appear to have sustained a schoolgirl crush on her throughout the years. So it was hardly surprising that Harvey's loquaciousness addressed to the whole table that evening fell on stony ground as far as Frances was concerned.

Deirdre, on the other hand, either joined in the laughter or, occasionally, at one of Harvey's wilder suggestions, exclaimed in disbelief. Harvey was not to be deflected by such minor interruptions, which, in any case, had a rather half-hearted ring, almost as if Deirdre didn't really care whether what he said was true or not. Even her laughter was like laughter of relief – relief that things were going well – rather than laughter provoked by genuine mirth.

One began to wonder what Deirdre felt about Harvey. Did she still idolize him as she had seemed to do at the time of their wedding or were the scales beginning to fall from her eyes? Even if the scales were falling from her eyes, did she really love him? She gave the impression of being set in a mould of acceptance, of being in a capsule of her own, out of which she could not reach and inside which she could not be touched. It would not be true to say that she appeared unhappy so much as rather lost. Puzzled, perhaps, at the way things turned out. No one ever dared to talk to her about babies and, so far as I know, she never, at that time, discussed her childlessness with anyone.

Others in our group had begun to have children and to these babies Deirdre was uniformly sweet.

Frances had two children, who were left at home with the nanny and to whom she referred as 'the little bores'. We all tittered rather uncomfortably, except for George, who looked as if he hadn't heard.

After dinner on that particular night we played silly party games and got fairly drunk. Harvey had always been rather a star at party games so that even during his farmer period he was prepared to cast binder twine to the winds and throw himself into charades or the acting game with gusto. I remember him on one occasion sitting on the floor, heedlessly chucking lighted matches around the room in an attempt to convey *Summer Lightning*. In those days, we all shared a cliquey and – on looking back – probably snobbish passion for Wodehouse, so that the answer was easy to guess despite the fact that Harvey's acting was more a vehicle for self-advertisement than a means of communication.

Deirdre – hardly surprisingly – took more of a back seat. In fact I always suspected that the whole thing was something like torture to her, although she never complained, but took part modestly and fairly ineffectively, passing her turn to someone else if she could possibly get away with it.

I was quite surprised when, after dinner, Frances, who had not appeared to be particularly enjoying herself, came to life during the acting game. There she stood in front of us all, pretty as a picture, neatly counting off the number of words on her fingers. She held up the five fingers of her left hand and the thumb on her right hand.

'Five! Seven! Eight!' people shouted indiscriminately. 'Six!'

at last someone called. Frances tossed back her lovely head and nodded enthusiastically, pointing at the same time to whoever had said 'Six'. She put her hands together in front of her as if in prayer, opened and shut them, and we all yelled, 'Book!'

Frances was still nodding as she held up this time three fingers from her left hand and jabbed at them forcefully with her right index finger. Third word.

She really did look delightful standing there, in the vanguard of fashion, dressed all in pink – pink dress, pink shoes – her skirt already more than an inch above the knee, hands held out on either side of her head as she twisted and turned, kissing the air so sweetly.

'*When the Kissing Had to Stop*!' someone bellowed frantically, whilst someone else scrambled to their feet and raced for the next clue. The game was always some kind of a race.

Amid cries of 'Frances, you were brilliant!' and 'Well done, Frances!', Frances returned demurely to her seat, smiling graciously round at everyone, for all the world like a fine actress taking a curtain call. 'It was a frightfully difficult one to do,' she said disingenuously, as all eyes turned to the next person, who was already frantically counting fingers in the middle of the room.

The game went on until late in the night with the clues becoming gradually more and more obscure, more and more difficult to act and more and more risqué. Frances and Harvey, in different ways, were both in their elements: Frances as the Venus de Milo and Harvey at one stage beginning to strip off his clothes as he thrust his pelvis crudely forward. How any of us guessed that he was acting *Love in a Cold Climate* I can't imagine, but luckily someone did before the whole thing got totally out of hand.

God only knows what time it was when we at last went to

bed. Halfway up the stairs I suddenly remembered that I had left a book I was reading in the drawing room. Seeing how late it was, I can't think why I bothered to go back for it since at that hour I was bound to go straight to sleep, but, for some reason, I turned and went downstairs again.

I could not have been more surprised when I pushed the drawing-room door open and saw Harvey and Frances sitting together on the club fender. There was nothing incriminating about what they were doing. They didn't have to jump apart, but merely turned to look at me, wondering perhaps why I had come back. Nevertheless, I felt uncomfortable and apologized gauchely for intruding.

Frances was sitting there, one pink shoe dangling casually from her big toe, saying nothing, looking innocent from under her eyelids.

Harvey, on the other hand and as usual, had something to say. But either I, because of my embarrassment, didn't hear what he was saying, or he, at that late hour, had nothing intelligible to say. Either way I didn't listen, but grabbed my book and ran. I could not have behaved more clumsily had I caught them *in flagrante* and yet they were doing nothing.

In bed at last, fuddled by alcohol, I wondered what it was that had so disturbed me. I thought about Deirdre and instantly fell asleep.

The next day we all got up late and as I woke, I remember thinking about the previous evening's scene. There had really been nothing to it and yet I felt uncomfortable.

In those days I thought of Harvey as splendid in his own way, gabbling on irrelevantly as he did. I knew him to be a bit of an ass, so that it never occurred to me, despite his boasting, to think that any woman apart from Deirdre would be likely to take him seriously. In fact I suppose that, if I thought about it at all, I would have considered him lucky to be married to someone solid and reliable like Deirdre who could act as an anchor to his indiscipline. Anyway, his boasting always seemed like mere bravado, so that the whole subject of Harvey's infidelity was treated as a joke by us all – including Deirdre, or so I fondly imagined. In any case, what was wrong with sitting on a club fender with someone?

Later in the morning I went with Deirdre to the vegetable garden to help her pick strawberries or raspberries or something for lunch. We strolled out across the lawn, under the copper beech towards the vegetable garden, which was surrounded by a thick hornbeam hedge. The way in was through an arch of hornbeam as carefully architected as if it were built of bricks and mortar. As we passed under the arch of neat green leaves, all thick and dense and tidy on their firm, twisted little branches, and came out into the sunlit garden, I suddenly caught my breath. Across the rows of lettuces and peas, barely camouflaged by the tall, grey foliage of the globe artichokes, Harvey and Frances were locked in an embrace.

Deirdre's little Cairn, sensing their presence, wagged his tail, barked joyfully and ran towards them. This time they did leap apart. Frances still in pink, a tiny rose-pink sack, as such dresses were called.

I could think of nothing to say. Neither, apparently, could Deirdre. I hoped that she might not have seen what I had seen; there was a closed expression on her face.

'Hello there, you two.' Harvey came striding towards us. 'I was just showing Frances the garden. Did you know that globe artichokes were originally imported to this country by Richard Coeur de Lion – who was incidentally the first king of England to use a handkerchief – after the Third Crusade – he regained Aquitaine for the crown and returned to England with the Giant Thistle of Aquitaine as a t-token of his success—'

'Codswallop,' I said.

Deirdre said nothing, but bent to cut a lettuce.

Chapter II

Harvey always says that he was unhappy when he first went away to school and there is little reason to doubt his word. At home he had been more indulged than most children of his generation and background. Where others – including his own older brother – were banished to the nursery, abandoned to nannies behind the green baize door, Harvey, from the earliest age, was always in the drawing room or even the dining room, at first dandled lovingly on his mother's knee, later sprawled languidly in a chair, encouraged to talk up, to interrupt the grown-ups and to try his wit. For some peculiar reason his mother always supposed his opinion on whatever subject to be of value.

She, poor woman, could never adjust to the cold light of Ayrshire where she had been taken in her early twenties by a much older husband and where she had given birth to two stillborn children in quick succession. A few years later, a healthy son was born, who seemed to surprise his mother by his ability to survive. Expecting him to follow her other little ones to the grave perhaps, she turned her back on him and refused ever to become attached to him, whereas when

Harvey came into the world fifteen years later, he immediately became the apple of his mother's eye. But people still saw her as a cold, unfeeling woman, which they partly attributed to her having been married apparently for ever to a dull old man who was both grumpy and uncommunicative. Hardness of hearing did nothing to alleviate either of these two conditions.

I remember Harvey's parents quite well. They both seemed incredibly old to me at the time, but his father really was old, crotchety, small, wizened by the time I met him and, like Harvey, very dark. His mother was much taller, so Harvey's height evidently came from her side of the family, which I thought odd because I knew her to be half French. Her maternal grandparents were Protestants from the Tarn.

Perhaps the particular brand of puritanism peculiar to French Protestants might have been expected to prepare the poor young bride to cope with the rigours of the long Scottish winters and the cold, late Victorian lodge which were to be her destiny. Her husband who was as English as English – brought up in Bedfordshire – inherited the property at an early age from a Scottish grandmother and instantly espoused the inheritance with a dour vigour, never thinking for one moment that he might exchange it for something in a neater, sweeter land. If anything, he bemoaned the fact that his lodge was not in the Highlands. Or so Harvey used to claim.

In any case Harvey's mother, who had spent much of her childhood in France, could never accustom herself to living in north Britain. She was a good-looking, elegant woman with pointed, rather French features for whom, surrounded by rain and mist and incarcerated as she was by gloomy, solid grey stone walls, life resembled a prison cell. She could never understand the romantic alliance which is said to exist between Scotland and France – Mary Stuart and all that. If anything – she used to tell Harvey – she pitied Mary Stuart, not so much for all the eighteen years she spent in captivity, as for having had to exchange the court at Fontainebleau for rude Scotland. She who had been queen of France.

Harvey always used to laugh at his parents as if they were not quite what he would have liked. But he laughed even more at his brother in a dismissive sort of way, almost daring anyone to stick up for him. Still would, for two pins. He has always, I suppose, been jealous of John.

The prep school to which Harvey was sent at the traditionally cruel, early age of eight was in the south of England, far from home. His father had been to the same school all those years before, as had John; so despite the privations of wartime and despite the fact that the school had changed hands and bore little resemblance to what it had formerly been, it was decided to send Harvey there too. Mrs Hotham, who doted so on her young son, must have been sorely distressed to lose him. At any event she wrote to him every day, recounting endless petty details of life in the brooding Scottish house and enumerating the numbers of days or weeks until his return.

When Harvey arrived for his first term, the Allies had already taken Sicily and were moving up through the foot of Italy; Mussolini had resigned and Italy had changed sides. Occasionally in her letters Mrs Hotham referred to such momentous events of world importance, but generally her communications were of a more domestic nature. Harvey himself, as a boy, was passionately interested in the war and bitterly jealous of schoolfellows whose fathers were young enough to be fighting.

To add insult to injury, John, at the age of eighteen, had declared himself a conscientious objector and so spent the war driving ambulances at the front. Harvey was not impressed. When asked if he had any brothers or sisters, he used at first to say that he had none, then, anxious to dazzle his audience, thinking only of the impact of the moment and heedless of what might have been said before, he decided to punish John and kill him off. John died many deaths. He was shot out of the sky at the Battle of Britain, drowned at Dunkirk, blown up in his tank at El Alamein, torpedoed in the Mediterranean. Sometimes he had even died before the war from a rare disease or a civilian accident, before the dreadful moment of his shame.

More articulate than most of his contemporaries and always prepared to use this talent as a screen for his real or imagined inadequacies, to put people off the scent – distract them from what they might otherwise have been thinking about him – Harvey was ever ready to recount John's last hour as, hurtling about the playground, his arms stretched out on either side of him he made a loud, whining, 'eee-owng' sort of noise in imitation of the Messerschmitt which finally blew his brother to smithereens.

Some of the more sensitive boys, or those whose fathers had indeed been killed, must have been a little surprised at Harvey's cavalier attitude to his courageous brother's demise. In any case he soon, as cocky new boys tend to do, made himself quite unpopular and hence unhappy.

At the age of eight Harvey was already tall for his age so that he suffered from the disadvantage of looking older than he was and therefore surprised people by his childish behaviour so that if, for instance, he cried, children and grown-ups alike tended to back away or to revile him for being a baby. And the trouble was that he cried a lot. He cried because he was homesick and because he missed his mother – although he would have died rather than admit that – and he cried because he was unpopular and because he was cold and because there was never enough to eat and the headmaster was a bully.

The only person at that time who ever seemed to be at all nice to him was the headmaster's young daughter who worked as a matron in the school. She was kind and pretty, fair-haired and gentle, and she mended your socks and was nice to you if you had a cold, but still he never felt that he could tell her quite how unhappy he was.

Despite his internal misery Harvey still tried to gain popularity – or at least to shield himself from his own feelings by extravagant expressions of a tireless fantasy. People laughed with him because he had a genuine ability to entertain, but behind his back they laughed at him and told each other that it was all lies. A few gullible boys sometimes believed him for a while but as he always contradicted his own stories, it was hard to keep faith for long.

The boys all believed that the headmaster was eating their rations; there seemed to be no other explanation for the fact that while they remained forever hungry, he was a fat man. This scenario alone was enough for Harvey's fertile imagination to feed on so that he recounted endless elaborate tales of having met the headmaster in the corridor and having intercepted him eating a chocolate éclair filled with real cream. The boys at school were only too ready to believe this kind of thing, although when he told his parents about it in the holidays, they were less receptive.

Harvey's mother could see that he was thin but this she tended to put down to the fact that he had, as they used to say, outgrown his strength. She fed him on Virol and cod-liver oil while he was at home and generally sent him back to school looking a little healthier. When the war ended, which must surely happen soon, then things would get better. There would be bananas again.

Sometimes she silently wished that she could keep her darling boy at home, not only because she missed him but because she knew him to be unhappy at school. She didn't believe his extravagant tales of starvation and torture but she sensed that they were founded somewhere in some sort of truth. What she did believe was that Harvey was talented, witty and brave, all of which, she thought, explained his tales of long-suffering and bravado. But of course there could be no breaking with tradition and boys had to grow into men, so off he went term after term, biting back the tears as he boarded the school train.

Harvey did eventually make a friend at school. Jeremy Webber was a pale, quiet little boy who, due to an accident at birth, was slightly lame and who, because of the merciless nature of children in gangs, was mocked and reviled by his fellows for what they perceived to be his embarrassing inadequacies. In fact he was a rather clever boy, with a warm heart, a certain amount of imagination and a quirky humour. So it was not merely because they were two loners that Webber and Harvey were thrown together. Webber indeed needed a friend, just as Harvey did, but Harvey made him laugh and they both, no doubt, recognized the spark of originality in the other.

There was nothing pusillanimous or false about Webber, so that once he and Harvey had got together, he would, undaunted, stick up for his friend, fight his corner and never deny the friendship. The gangs gradually came to respect this and life became easier for the two boys. Soon Harvey came to depend on Jeremy, not only to laugh at his stories and to champion him, but as a sparring partner or stooge. No doubt Harvey felt himself to be superior to Webber in every way. He who towered above his small friend was already showing remarkable promise on the cricket field, while poor Jeremy watched from the sidelines, excused from games because of a misshapen hip. And Harvey, although he wept for home, was a bold and courageous sportsman, athletic and unafraid, always ready to dive recklessly from the highest diving board, somersaulting through the air.

Webber, it appeared, was never jealous of Harvey's prowess. Perhaps nature had compensated him for his physical disability with an equable disposition which gave him the ability to remain curiously unscathed by the world's arbitrary cruelties. Other boys still teased them, laughed at the incongruity of the two friends, and sniggered behind their backs, but for Harvey and Webber the sting had been drawn and as they went about together, inseparable, they presented a united front, although it may indeed not have been obvious to everyone that in reality it was the little one who protected the big one.

Harvey took Webber to stay with his parents in Ayrshire and learned to call him Jeremy, but he only took him there once because the experience had not, he felt, been a success. Mrs Hotham was clearly unimpressed by her son's little guest and rather disappointed at the appearance of what she regarded as a sickly child masquerading as her precious boy's best friend, where instead she would have expected to find a tall, blond, fresh-faced, healthy, sporting child. She couldn't imagine what Harvey could see in that poor little mite. As is often the way with adoring parents, she interpreted her son's motives to suit the image she had created of him for herself, and thus put it about that Harvey had such a soft heart that he had in his kindness befriended this poor cripple and brought him home out of charity.

Jeremy cannot have been quite insensitive to the disregard of Harvey's mother – or father for that matter – but he never complained to anyone and always maintained that he had had a wonderful time on his one and only visit to Scotland, although it must have been obvious to him that Harvey, embarrassed by his friend in front of his parents' barely disguised disapproval, became somewhat distant and supercilious. But Jeremy, not to be wrong-footed by such futile snobbery, loyally continued to invite Harvey back to his home in Somerset. Jeremy's father owned a shirt factory in Taunton and the family lived in an agreeable red stone village house on the edge of the Quantock hills. When Harvey first went to stay there he was taken quite by surprise, having always imagined that the only real countryside in Britain was in Scotland.

From Taunton, in those long-ago days, he used to take a branch-line train which puffed its way sedately through the valley towards the sea. Sheep and cows grazed peacefully on either side of the line as Harvey looked out at the gently inviting hills to the right and paused perhaps, if Harvey ever paused, to wonder at the redness of the earth, maybe even at the softness of the light. In any case, he has always retained a strange affection for that part of England, eventually living there for some years.

Jeremy's mother, who collected Harvey from the little local station in an old leather-upholstered Rover, was slightly awed by the arrival of her son's ebullient friend and consequently treated Harvey rather as if he were a visiting celebrity, laughing exaggeratedly at his swaggering tomfoolery, and repeatedly asking him what he would like to do. Jeremy, clearly delighted by the impression his friend made, felt his status in the family had immediately improved.

It was not just the beauty of the Quantock hills, nor Mrs Webber's extravagant laughter and respectful treatment of him that attracted Harvey back to stay on more than one occasion with his friend, so much as the fact that Jeremy was the youngest of five children, the four eldest all being girls.

Harvey, who knew no other girls, became obsessed with the concept of the Misses Webber, with what he regarded as the fourness of them, so that in his imagination they acquired the kind of four-persons-in-one, indivisible quality usually attributed only to the Holy Trinity. Perhaps he sometimes thought he preferred Caroline, the youngest girl, particularly when she came cantering off the hills on her little strawberry roan, cheeks shining with rosy health, red pigtails flying, puppy fat encased in tight, sweaty jodhpurs. At other times it was one of the more sophisticated older sisters about whom he dreamed – Rosemary, the pale, thin one with large breasts who looked so perfect in her mother's blue and white New Look cotton dress. But whichever one he thought about, she was inextricably entwined in his imagination with the other three. To a certain extent, he became obsessed with them all, weaving in his mind ever more exotic fantasies involving them and persuading himself that they, in turn, were each dreaming of him, perhaps dreaming of teaching him something about the mysteries of sex.

Back at school he boasted about these girls, quite regardless of the fact that they were his best friend's sisters who had received him with nothing but good-mannered amiability during the holidays. Harvey at twelve was a large, precocious boy who could easily have passed for fourteen or fifteen and who was already longing for female flesh, his mind ever turned towards the possibility of the unlikeliest of brief encounters which might begin to satisfy his curiosity if not his lust. In Harvey's imagination he had fondled the breasts of each of the Misses Webber in turn, had kissed them in the stables or lying in the heather on the hills, he had watched them undressing, sometimes by meanly peeping through a keyhole, at others with their connivance, invited by one or other of them into the privacy of the bedroom.

Of course all the boys gossiped madly about Harvey's supposed adventures, half believing them half the time, furiously jealous and curious, too, about such insights as there were into Jeremy's home life. While some wanted to believe all these stories, there were those who dismissed them out of hand as typical of Harvey's usual lies, and there were also those who wanted Harvey undone. Here was an excellent chance to make trouble, even to break up the apparently invincible friendship between the two boys.

It was soon reported back to Webber that Harvey had been spreading salacious stories about his eldest sister, Angela who, at the age of nineteen, had her eye on a nice young local estate agent, recently demobbed, whom she in fact later married. It was hardly likely that she should have paid the slightest attention to a dirty-minded, overgrown twelve-year-old friend of her little brother's. Jeremy was angry when he heard what was being said. He hated to hear his sisters spoken of in such vile terms, so lost his temper and hit the boy who had spread the unwelcome news, who, in turn, split on Jeremy for thumping him, and then said it wasn't his fault if he'd got it wrong; perhaps it was Susan, not Angela, who'd shown Harvey her tits in the barn down in Somerset. Jeremy felt like thumping him again but he was already in deep trouble because, being a decent boy who would never have dreamed of telling tales and who would have been disgusted to repeat such horrible things about Angela – or Susan, for that matter – he had never divulged the reason for his unprecedented attack on Winterbottom Minor.

Jeremy didn't want to believe that such horrible stories had really originated with the friend he had trusted enough to take home; but although he wanted to blame the other boys for inventions which he could have borne more easily had they sprung from the daily currency of malice to which he had become all too well accustomed, he had a nasty feeling that Harvey, with his tireless need to invent, was in fact at the root of the trouble. To begin with, Harvey was probably the only boy who knew the names of all his sisters; he was certainly the only boy who knew anything about a barn at the back of the house. For a while Jeremy made excuses to keep away from Harvey. He felt hurt, betrayed and a little bitter so that he could hardly bear to talk to him, but eventually a desire to have it out overcame these other feelings and he decided on a confrontation. Besides he had come to think that the only way to put an end to the rumours, which were still rife, was to say something. He wanted to fight but, what with his diminutive size and crooked hip, he realized he would be terrifically disadvantaged against the huge, athletic Harvey.

In the end, of course, it did come to a fight – one which ended in some sort of Pyrrhic victory for Jeremy, who, bruised and battered in the fray with Harvey, emerged for all the world to see as victor. Harvey never once admitted his guilt to his friend, nor apologized, but went around the school instead inventing some rigmarole to explain why he and his best friend had been involved in what turned out to be quite a nasty scrap.

Jeremy got himself into terrible trouble over the whole episode and gained a reputation among the staff for aggression. The headmaster wrote to his parents and he was gated for the rest of the term, whereas Harvey was merely given a severe warning and reprimanded for fighting with someone so much smaller than himself. On the other hand, the nasty stories about Harvey and the Webber sisters began to die a natural death. For one thing Harvey had had a fright. He did not want to lose his friend and be left on his own again and, since he had developed a healthy respect for Jeremy, he recognized the need to tread carefully in future. After all, besotted as he was with Angela and Susan and the rest, he sincerely hoped to be invited back to Somerset. Next time who knows what might happen in the barn or on the hills. So with his usual belief in his own charm, in his ability to talk himself out of any tight corner and in his powers of persuasion, he began to evolve a new scenario for what had passed.

He swore to Jeremy on the Holy Bible that he would never ever have dreamed of saying anything untrue about the sisters, the four of whom he thought to be completely beautiful and perfect in every way. He had certainly talked about them and told some other boys about how pretty they were, but the rest was all filthy lies invented by one particular sworn enemy of his. Harvey was appalled to think that for one moment Jeremy could have believed that he, Harvey, would ever have said such dreadful things about people whom – he did assure Jeremy – he almost regarded as sisters himself.

Faute de mieux Jeremy decided to believe Harvey and so eventually not only forgave him, but even apologized for having picked a fight. But when the holidays next came round he nevertheless felt a reluctance to invite him home again. The whole episode had left Jeremy with a niggling feeling of discomfort.

The sisters, though, were rather sorry not to see Harvey coming back; he had amused them and they liked having him around with their younger brother. Jeremy's mother was sorry too, as she, not unnaturally, worried about her boy and sensed that his disability might have been originally what stood in the way of his making friends; but when she urged him to invite Harvey again, she met with a blank wall of refusal only. Jeremy never said anything whatsoever to the detriment of his friend, but without ever giving a reason, he steadfastly determined not to ask him home again.

Up in Ayrshire, Mrs Hotham was relieved by what she supposed to be the end of her son's friendship with the little boy she regarded as so dreary; she was certainly quite unable to understand what on earth he might have found to amuse him so much in Somerset – nor could she imagine for the life of her why it was that Harvey would go on saying how much he wanted to go back there and how sure he was that Jeremy would invite him again in the summer. Apart from anything else, she must have felt jealous. She, who so adored her boy, wanting him permanently by her side, must have bitterly resented his longing to leave home during the all-too-short holidays.

With lavish presents and pledges of new bicycles and airguns, with promises that he should have all his favourite food, that the best strawberries and biggest greenhouse peaches should be kept for him, she did her best to cement him to her side. But Harvey only dreamed licentiously about the Misses Webber, left his new bicycle outside in the rain and idly shot out the window panes in the potting shed with his air rifle.

Mrs Hotham decided that her son had outgrown his prep school, that it was high time he moved on. She looked forward to his going to public school. She somehow did not expect that he and Jeremy would be going on to the same school, so the enforced separation would put an end to what had from the start been an improbable alliance. At his public school Harvey would find a better sort of boy. She was most displeased when she discovered herself to be mistaken and learned that indeed the two boys would be starting out together again the following year.

At school, despite the drama concerning his sisters, Jeremy remained as inseparable as ever from Harvey. He was just very careful whenever he mentioned the subject of home, and if Harvey dropped hints – which he frequently did – Jeremy merely brushed them aside or pretended not to have understood their inference.

Harvey was never really sure why Jeremy reacted in this way, since, sublimely confident of his power to dissemble, he had persuaded himself that Jeremy believed him to be quite innocent with regard to the stories about the girls, which had so unfortunately been circulating. He also supposed that although rumour and gossip had long since moved on to concern themselves with other, more topical matters, there must remain somewhere in the consciousness of his fellows the idea that he, Harvey, had experienced some rich excitement and thrilling adventure which they could only dream of. This he found most gratifying and in order to keep a healthy respect for his sexual prowess alive, he invented a Scottish girl called Fiona and a whole new series of banal and squalid little escapades to accompany her.

Eventually the five years were up and the time came for the two boys to leave their preparatory school, by which time they were both bored and longing to move on to greater things. They sat their Common Entrance and Jeremy, who was bright and who paid attention to his books, passed with high marks. Harvey, who, when he wasn't thinking about sex, was thinking about cricket, did rather less well. Mrs Hotham, disappointed in the outcome, blamed the school.

That summer – the summer of 1948 – Harvey went abroad for the first time. His mother, forever pining for her childhood haunts in the Tarn, decided to take him with her on what had become her yearly visit to an aunt and uncle who inhabited a decrepit château near Castres. The war years had kept Mrs Hotham in Scotland and since the end of the war, with the travel allowance being so small, it was at first impossible to consider taking Harvey abroad. Mr Hotham had no desire for such trips. But, soon, as various relations started coming to London from France, it was possible to arrange a private system of financial exchange which made travelling between the two countries infinitely easier.

Harvey was delighted by the prospect of his foreign trip. Apart from anything else, he felt it would undoubtedly give him some standing when he arrived at his new school. No other boy he knew had ever been abroad. But he hadn't bargained for quite how difficult life can be in a country where one can't speak the language, and furthermore, being Harvey, he had fondly imagined that he could already speak French. After all, he had not only learned it at school, but he had a French grandmother and over the years his mother had taught him a few phrases at home. *Madame Souris a une maison. Où sont mes souliers?* And a few others.

When Harvey and his mother arrived in the decrepit château after a long overnight train journey from Paris, it was raining. Harvey was bitterly disappointed, having always presumed that the sun shone all the time in France. A severe elderly woman who turned out to be his great-aunt met them at the little local station in a pre-war Citroën and drove them at a snail's pace the few miles back to the house, jabbering all the time in an incomprehensible tongue to Mrs Hotham who, Harvey couldn't help noticing, looked very happy.

He was not at all happy, but tired and bored. When they finally reached the château they were taken into a large, cold, panelled dining room where about twelve people of all ages were having breakfast. Mrs Hotham kissed everyone on both cheeks. One small child was crying. Harvey didn't blame it; he, too, felt utterly miserable and very large as he was introduced to this medley of new cousins. There were two bright-eyed boys of about his own age who were detailed to look after him, both of whom were half his size.

On the way upstairs to be shown their bedrooms Harvey noticed on the landing a bucket into which water was dripping from the ceiling; some of the drops, however, landed outside the bucket, giving the boards around it a sodden appearance. In the only bathroom there was a smell of drains, and when you pulled the lavatory plug there started up such a shaking and a groaning in the pipes that it seemed as if the entire château might explode. If you went to the lavatory, the whole household knew you had been.

The whole household in fact consisted of more than the original dozen whom Harvey had encountered at breakfast. As that first morning wore on, more and more people appeared like creatures out of the woodwork. It was quite impossible to work out who was whose wife or mother or sister, as they gabbled away in their horrid alien tongue. Harvey noticed one woman with a huge protuberant belly and stared at her agog. Later Mrs Hotham explained that Tante Anne was expecting a baby. To the best of his knowledge, Harvey had never seen a pregnant woman before.

In the kitchen one very old, witchlike character in black, with bow legs and a single discoloured tooth, worked away indefatigably preparing meals for the hordes, helped at intervals by the women of the house.

After a few days, during which time Harvey longed to be back at home, things began to improve. For one thing it stopped raining and for another the two boys of Harvey's age stopped fighting and instead took him outside and taught him to play boules and volleyball, both of which pastimes were better than hanging around the house with nothing to do, understanding nothing. Harvey, always at a loss unless he could resort to chatter, fabrication and imagery as a means of beguiling those among whom he found himself, soon discovered that the only substitutes for language in the present company were humour and a willingness to join in. Since he was a competitive sportsman at the best of times, joining in came naturally to him: at boules, at volleyball and on the crumbling, rutted tennis court.

The children rode bicycles and swam in the river and ate picnic lunches, and Harvey learned to laugh with them and push and make silly noises. Of course he learned how to swear in French and he taught the others how to swear in English and, deprived as he was of articulacy, he still managed to endear himself to his cousins.

'*Le petit anglais*,' the grown-ups decided, '*s'amuse beaucoup*.' And Mrs Hotham was happy. Far from Scotland and far from Mr Hotham.

After a month, when the time came to return home, Harvey really had learned a few first smatterings of French; he had also experienced an inexplicable sense of freedom which he could probably not have rationalized to himself but which reminded him more than anything of staying in the Quantocks with Jeremy.

But now, at last, Jeremy's sisters had relinquished their hold over Harvey's imagination. Thinking about them, he decided they were dull and frumpy and could never compare to the sophistication and beauty of what he had seen in France. In fact there had been no girl cousins of his own age but he had allowed his thoughts to linger over a young, newly married woman – one of his mother's cousins – so slim and brown with a big nose, an elegant neck, a dark, shiny chignon and a husband who adored her. How Harvey envied that husband! He fantasized about killing him in a duel or knocking him out with a cricket ball hit for a six and tumbling inexorably out of the sky – then Tante Marie-France would be his . . . He begged his mother to bring him back to the Tarn the following year. She wanted nothing more.

Back in Scotland, Harvey found himself without playmates and with only his parents for an audience. His father barely pretended to listen to his traveller's tales, being more concerned with his own affairs and the running of an ailing estate, and his mother – much as she doted on him – was hardly likely to be impressed by his anecdotes or to believe his exaggerations. He looked forward to the new term and the new school.

Harvey, with his carefree, lively chatter, his prowess at games and his heedless manner, found it easier to make friends at public school than he had done at his prep school. Perhaps he had learned better to judge his audiences. However it may have been, shyer, more diffident boys than he were impressed by what they saw as his urbanity and, without really getting to know him, were initially glad to shelter under his wing. He was funny; he seemed grown-up and clever, had arrived with a brilliant reputation as a cricketer and, unlike most of the others, he had been abroad. One boy boasted of having spent the war in America. Before long Harvey was in the under-fourteen rugby team and had collected a small gang of admiring acolytes.

The mythical Scottish Fiona of yesteryear was replaced by French Fifi. Harvey swore on the Holy Bible that that really was her name and that she was up to all sorts of French tricks to make the imaginations of uncouth English schoolboys boggle. Tante Marie-France was too precious to Harvey for him to want to share her with others or to tarnish her name by publicizing his fantasies and all their attendant filth. Fifi would do fine. Harvey claimed to have a photograph of her in the nude which he intimated he might show to people for a fee. He hadn't decided quite what to do if someone did offer to ante up.

Jeremy, who had spent an uneventful summer at home with his family, was more daunted than Harvey appeared to be by the new school, but overjoyed to see his friend again. He was a little hurt when Harvey didn't seem quite to reciprocate, but put it down to the fact that everything was strange and that Harvey, being Harvey, needed to impress. He was confident that before long they would settle down to their old, inseparable ways. For his part he didn't find it any easier to make friends now than he had before; he was self-conscious and, as other boys found him a little odd, they were loath to make overtures to him. He waited patiently for Harvey and in the meantime was lonely.

But Harvey was on the crest of a wave, quite full of himself – no longer needing Jeremy. In fact, embarrassed to think that Jeremy had once been his friend, he was reluctant even to admit the friendship to his new cronies. He had moved on.

A few weeks into the first term Jeremy overheard a boy talking to Harvey. 'Wasn't Webber at prep school with you?' he asked. 'Bit of a weed, isn't he?'

And Harvey replied, 'Yes, but I hardly knew him. We never went around together.'

Chapter III

Perhaps Deirdre blotted the memory of Harvey and Frances kissing in the vegetable garden out of her mind, or perhaps she just thought of it as something which had happened casually in summer as the result of a minor flirtation and in a light-hearted moment of fun. However it may have been, I was quite surprised to learn later that year that she and Harvey were going on holiday to Tuscany with Frances and George. They did at some point ask me to go along with them, but I was unable to get away at the time and anyway could probably not have afforded it.

What I heard about it all afterwards made me quite glad that I hadn't been able to go.

By then there already seemed to be trouble brewing. Harvey was clearly bored stiff with farming and was idly looking around for some other way of amusing himself and replenishing his rapidly dwindling fortune. Deirdre too seemed down, almost as though the depression which had hit her during the early days of marriage had revisited her. No one really knew whether it was her relationship with Harvey that was getting at her or whether she was made unhappy by her continuing childlessness. Most people probably presumed it to be a combination of both these things.

Harvey was talking of selling the farm. Sometimes he thought of selling the land only and keeping the house and at others he just wanted to be rid of the whole bang shoot. Deirdre's opinion seemed to have no bearing on the matter whatsoever. It was as if she were waiting patiently in the wings for some sort of divine signal as to what her future might be. She had retreated even further into herself and spoke very little.

I remember wondering how she and Frances got on together and even asked her how she thought they would manage in Italy at such close quarters for so long. She merely smiled and said she liked Frances. Perhaps she thought that Frances's vitality might communicate itself to her.

Deirdre, since her Venetian honeymoon, had learned a bit about the Italian Renaissance and could, I'm sure, hold her own with Harvey or anyone else for that matter. She'd developed a certain enthusiasm for art history, if all the art books lying around at Shackles were anything to go by. I very much doubt that they had much to do with Harvey, who has always been more of a talker than a reader – and a bluffer at that.

Not that Deirdre ever mentioned what she'd read – least of all did she show off about it – but just mulled it over in her mind. I remember thinking, though, that the Tuscan trip might jolt her out of her depression since in an unexpected way, and despite George and Frances, it did seem to be more her thing than Harvey's for once. But Harvey was the one, of course, to hold forth about it all the time; to bombard us with garbled information about the Guelphs and the Ghibellines and to tell us about the sex lives of the Medicis. Most of us were unlikely to know much about the Guelphs and

Ghibellines, having little, if any, idea of what they each represented; but for clarification Harvey was hardly the right person to turn to, ready though he might have been with improbable anecdotes about the period.

Deirdre told me later that the first week of the holiday, spent in Florence, was wonderful, that she hadn't been so happy for a long time. She was excited and totally absorbed by everything she saw, completely indefatigable, never tiring of tramping through the stony streets into the next church, round the next museum. She'd discovered about comfortable shoes since her honeymoon – learned to put art before fashion. Not so Frances, who was tripping around the place in stylish little psychedelic sandals and twisting her ankle on every other cobblestone, flaking early in the day and retiring to the *pensione*, the straw market or even to the expensive jeweller's shops on the Ponte Vecchio when Deirdre was still full of energy.

George and Harvey, when they had had enough, usually said they were off to look for English newspapers. Deirdre imagined them sitting in a bar, silently side by side behind the *Express* or the *Mail* – whatever they could find – sipping Carpano and Seltz. For her own part, she was quite happy alone. Happier really than when she was with the others. She could go at her own pace, stop and stare, gawp and daydream and move on as she pleased. Deirdre can gaze far longer than anyone else I know at a single picture.

By the end of the day she was tired, but elated and ready to enjoy supper with the others in a noisy trattoria. For once she seemed to be getting on quite well with Harvey, who was less irritable than usual and clearly enjoying the company of both George and Frances. She felt so much more positive than she had for such a long time that she had begun to think about taking drawing lessons when she got home. She didn't want to sink back into her customary inertia. But then, what with Harvey talking of selling the house, with no particular idea of what he wanted to do or where he wanted to go next, the future for Deirdre must have seemed rather uncertain, to say the least.

Harvey, apparently, was on some sort of a high all the time they were away and, if the subject of the proposed move was so much as mentioned, he dismissed it airily with a wave of the hand and straight away began to talk of something else. Deirdre presumably felt no urge to prolong a discussion on the subject while she was enjoying herself and while there was nothing to be done about it. She would face the problem when she had to.

Sometimes I believe she felt embarrassed by Harvey's unrestrained flow of chatter. He talked about everything and nothing, evidently unable to draw breath for a single minute, with no rhyme or reason to half of what he was saying, jumping from one subject to another, inventing preposterous lies, revealing the most private if imagined details of other people's sex lives, of their financial situations, assuring everyone all the time that what he said was absolutely true, that he did happen to know about it all from first-hand information. I have myself occasionally seen Harvey in that mode and when he talks like this he gives the impression of being high on some kind of hallucinatory drug, quite unable to control the mindless drivel he is spouting, no longer able to amuse and charm with his rigmaroles of quasi-nonsense as he is able to do at his best.

Deirdre must have wondered what on earth George and Frances could possibly be making of Harvey in this overexcited frame of mind and she must have wondered whether or not it would mean the end of a flourishing friendship. But as she absorbed the beauty of Renaissance Italy, drank in the glories of Ghirlandaio and Masaccio, returned day after day to the Pitti palace or the Uffizi, she may have put such concerns on one side.

After a week they moved on to Siena and then spent the last few days in Arezzo. By the time they left Florence, Deirdre was just beginning to feel that she couldn't take in very much more and that she would have to go at a more leisurely pace.

One wonders what the relationship between the two women must have been like at this stage. Frances, apparently so much more sophisticated than Deirdre, certainly more sure of herself, quite competitive and a great deal more egocentric, had acquired a smattering of superficial knowledge about a great many things which made it possible for her, to some extent, to breeze her way through life, smiling and pleasing. She probably never really let Deirdre impinge on her and yet there must have been times when they were alone together and talked.

Deirdre remembers Frances being quite clever about what they had seen, discussing clothes a good deal, and people, but she admits that she never felt she was getting to know her any better as the days passed.

And what part did George play? George has always been something of an enigma: so successful in banking, so lackadaisical in his private life. I can imagine him enjoying the sightseeing in a casual sort of way, perhaps sometimes genuinely moved by a work of art, but never prepared to say so, quiet almost to the point of taciturnity, not wanting to do too much in any one day, sitting in the sun reading – always reading. George is one of those people who will read anything – for whom the written word is an absolute concomitant of happiness. He is without doubt one of the best-read people I have ever known, but such is his need for literature that in a crisis anything will do, from the popular press to the information on a packet of cigarettes or the instructions contained in a box of pills or insect-repellent cream. I can just picture him, intently, with his long fingers, pulling that thin white sheet out of a box, opening it up carefully and squinting at the small print: *posologie: 1 à 2 comprimés le soir* . . . Reading every word – in French, in English, in German – totally engrossed.

It is difficult to imagine what he and Deirdre could have had in common, although she may well have found him an agreeable contrast to Harvey. He, one can only suppose, allowed Harvey's excitable monologue to flow over him unheeded and yet he must initially have been amused by it for the friendship to have existed at all.

In fact Deirdre has always claimed that she got on well with George. On that holiday she liked the way he sat and read, producing a new book almost every day from an enormously heavy canvas bag which was part of his luggage. Sometimes it would be a Perry Mason thriller or the biography of some nineteenth-century statesman, at others an abstruse work of German literature or a scientific thesis on the origins of the universe. He and Frances generally seemed to accept each other as part of the furniture, barely exchanging a word, yet occasionally and unexpectedly making each other laugh. George, usually so silent, has a quick and ready wit, his one-liners being produced in a perfect deadpan fashion to which Frances's reaction has always been immediate.

Towards the end of the holiday, Deirdre now admits, she began to feel rather irritated by Frances's cheerful acceptance of Harvey's wilder chatter and by her attitude towards him. Frances, who was, after all, a perfectly intelligent woman, appeared to be quite enchanted by everything Harvey said, to believe it and to admire it. Deirdre wondered if she was merely being polite, or perhaps she was just a much sillier woman than might have been supposed. In any case she continued to flirt like mad with Harvey, who appeared to be perpetually nervous and who continued to gabble. George, it seems, paid very little attention to either of them, but just went on reading.

Although Deirdre was irritated by Frances, she didn't in any way feel threatened, partly because she knew that flirting was part of Frances's stock-in-trade and partly because it seemed totally inconceivable that anyone could possibly be taking Harvey seriously in his present frame of mind. All the same, by the time the four of them bade each other a fond farewell at Heathrow Airport, swearing to go together next year to Calabria or perhaps Burgundy, she was rather relieved that they could now go their separate ways.

All the way home in the car which they had left parked at the airport, Harvey continued to talk. In a crazy sort of way he had suddenly become remarkably attentive to Deirdre, talking to her as he had not usually done of late, in a confiding, almost flattering tone. Deirdre at once felt herself retreating, going back into her shell, afraid perhaps of the future, afraid of this neurotic man beside her who seemed unable to find any inner peace and in whose hands her destiny lay.

For a few days after their return to Shackles, Harvey never mentioned the possibility of moving and life continued much as it had done before, with Deirdre delighted to be reunited with her precious dog and still eager to take up drawing lessons. Drawing lessons would be something to do to fill the long empty days. She made enquiries locally and even enrolled in some course or other. Harvey was hardly ever at home – always dashing off to London on some excuse to which Deirdre paid little heed, and coming back, head in air, as cheerful as a cricket, and as often as not bearing some little trinket or delicacy for his wife. Deirdre wondered what she could have done to deserve such sudden attention.

It was a little time before the bombshell broke. Deirdre was going to her art lessons and seemed to be enjoying them but she couldn't help noticing that Harvey was leaving her alone at home more and more often and for longer and longer periods. He was quite ignoring the farm, had sold the Guernsey herd and was letting everything slide generally so that she was bound to begin to grow anxious. She must have known that they could not simply drift on in this sort of half-world, communicating very little, neither of them really knowing where they were heading – where they would even be living in a year's time. She realized that she ought to be saying something to try to pin Harvey down, but she, of all people, must have been fully aware of quite how impossible Harvey could be to pin down. Besides he seemed so cheerful – was still on a high from the trip to Italy – that she felt reluctant to interfere with that mood.

Even when she was told by a so-called friend that Frances and Harvey had been seen together in London on a day when he had categorically told her that he had been elsewhere, she failed to put two and two together and merely presumed that there must have been some mistake. She must have known that she and Harvey were not really happy – perhaps that they never had been – but young and green as she still was at the time, her mind must have been clouded by some sort of swirling fog through which she was unable to see either the reality of her situation or how, in any way, she could alter things. Perhaps her emotions were paralysed in such a fashion that she was prevented from seeing things clearly or from taking any kind of action which would release her from the limbo in which she was living. The art classes, which took place two mornings a week at the local technical college, hardly constituted a life, and in the evenings she was surely lonely sitting there night after night, endlessly drawing her little Cairn terrier.

Then Harvey would return home so full of bounce and prattle, full of stories of where he had been and what he had been up to, to which she barely listened, perhaps from some unconscious or semi-conscious fear of what she might hear, or of recognizing his lies for what they were. And then the weekends would come and once again the house would fill up with friends and George and Frances would be there, and then, after a while, only Frances, because George had so much work to catch up on.

One weekend when Frances came on her own, I was there. There were no other guests on that occasion and I couldn't help wondering how Deirdre could bear what was going on so blatantly under her nose. Frances and Harvey had eyes only for each other – and ears too, for that matter. Anything that Deirdre or I wanted to communicate to either of them had to be repeated at least three times, while they laughed loudly at each other's jokes and oohed and aahed at each other's passing remarks. Harvey certainly seemed to be totally oblivious to anything but Frances and completely unaware of the figure he was cutting, which, to say the least, was ludicrous.

I, truly not knowing, as they say, where to put myself, retreated into a gauche silence which could hardly have helped Deirdre, and spent most of the weekend with my nose in a book: the said book – whatever it may have been – acting as a kind of barricade between myself and everything that was going on around me.

Frances, I couldn't help noticing, was looking enchantingly pretty; her high-pitched, clear, merry laugh tinkled like a bell, bursting at all times from a pearly throat as she, glowing with health and joy, flaunted herself unselfconsciously in the full knowledge of the admiration she was inspiring. Occasionally she threw a sideways comment at Deirdre as if half remembering that this woman was her hostess and, as such, deserved passing recognition.

At lunch on Saturday Deirdre announced that she wanted to spend the afternoon at some sort of local arts and crafts fair where someone from her drawing classes had a stall. She wondered if any of us would like to go too. It wasn't a particularly nice day and there didn't seem to be much else to do. Frances immediately claimed that she was tired and had a bit of a headache – a headache which her lively behaviour up until that moment certainly belied – and that she would rather spend a quiet afternoon at the house. Harvey said that he was busy – would have loved to have gone but unfortunately had to see a man about a mowing machine. First Deirdre had heard of it.

I was left feeling like a pig in the middle, embarrassed to go with Deirdre, thus conniving with Harvey and Frances in their desire to remain behind together and so possibly increasing what I imagined to be Deirdre's suffering, but neither did I want to stay. I really didn't know what to do but eventually – tactlessly or even unkindly perhaps – I left Deirdre to go to her craft fair on her own.

Deirdre's car had hardly disappeared down the drive before Frances said with her tinkling little laugh, which was beginning to get on my nerves, that she thought she would go for a siesta.

Harvey unwound himself from the sofa in which he was sitting and announced that he'd better go and see this man about a mowing machine.

'You be all right?' he addressed me, without bothering to look at me and certainly with no care for the answer. Then he began to speak expansively about mowing machines, standing in front of me, long legs apart, waving his arms about enthusiastically as he talked. His enthusiasm, though, was to die just as suddenly as it had been born, and he dropped his arms with a 'Must be off' and strode from the room. A few moments later I heard his light tread ascending the stairs. So far as I knew that was to be the last anyone heard of a man-about-a-mowing-machine.

I, feeling somewhat forlorn and despite the drizzling grey day, took myself for a short walk intending to return to the fireside with a book for the rest of the afternoon. I remember the little Cairn terrier refusing sullenly to accompany me, preferring instead to wait obstinately by the front door for his mistress's return. He had a second sense, that dog. Deirdre was going to need him when she got back.

What happened later that afternoon had the makings of a French farce.

When she got to the village hall in which the craft fair was taking place, Deirdre found it to be full of rubbish, so she looked around briefly, then, as a sop to her friend, bought some banal little flower paintings in tacky wooden frames, themselves decorated with coyly painted butterflies and bees, and decided to leave. She thought she could hang the paintings in the spare bathroom with impunity and hoped her friend would never ask to see them. Perhaps she could even give them to one of her sisters for Christmas.

Suddenly the whole atmosphere of the village hall, crowded as it was with so many optimistic, innocent amateurs, their lifeless paintings, their dried flowers, bamboo recorders and mud-coloured pottery, had filled her with a deep despair so that she had to go away immediately.

On the way home she got to within half a mile of Shackles when the car began to swerve and then to bump along unevenly so that she realized she had a puncture. She managed to drive the car on to the verge, where she planned to leave it until she could get someone to come and change the wheel for her. Then – for no apparent reason – gathered up her newly acquired flower paintings before setting out to walk the rest of the way home.

It's funny to think of Deirdre all those years ago leaving that car on the side of the road, as nowadays she would take a pride in changing the wheel herself – but then that was all long before she became interested in doing things – before Deirdre really came into her own: before she learned how to look after herself, how to unblock a drain, change a washer or, for that matter, fix a power plug.

Anyway, as Deirdre came walking unexpectedly up the drive with her ridiculous bundle of flower paintings under her arm, a man appeared as if from nowhere, stealthily walking across the gravel in front of the house, dressed in overalls. A green bicycle which Deirdre didn't recognize was leaning awkwardly up against the wall by the dining-room window, slightly crushing some lavender bushes. Peculiar. It flitted through the surface of her mind without stopping to be registered, that a man-about-a-mowing-machine was unlikely to come by bike. But being more concerned by the ennui that had seized her than by anything so tedious as a mowing machine, she only wanted to hand the man over to Harvey as quickly as possible.

'Ah,' she said, 'you must be looking for my husband. Do come in.'

The man said nothing but meekly, in his Hush Puppies, followed her through the front door into the house, where the little terrier leaped joyfully to greet his mistress before turning to welcome the stranger. Deirdre patted the dog absentmindedly.

'I bought these,' she said, and deposited her pictures in a heap on the hall table. 'And I've had a puncture just outside the village.'

The man advanced gingerly into the hall and craned his neck over the table and the paintings, without looking at what he was seeing. He had a strange, absent expression on his face, almost as if he were occupied only with some arcane inner world of his own.

'Do you believe in God?' he asked.

Deirdre hardly heard him: certainly didn't consciously receive into her intelligence what had been said. Indeed she heard without hearing as the man looked without seeing.

'Wait here,' she said. 'I'll go and find my husband for you.'

My walk had taken longer than I had originally meant it to. Even when the weather is dull and grey, it can be nicer outside than in – certainly less depressing – and so what had been intended as a brisk twenty minutes round the village had been extended to include a decent walk through woods and fields. As I turned back through the gates of Shackles, I was slightly surprised to see an odd-looking fellow on a green bicycle coming towards me down the drive. He was talking animatedly to himself, almost with an intense passion, as he swerved unsteadily from side to side. Under his left arm he was carrying what looked like three or four small pictures. I wondered who he might be. Hardly the man-about-a-mowing-machine, I thought: I'd never really believed in him, in any case, but there had been no mention of anyone else coming during the afternoon.

I said good afternoon as he passed, but the man on the bicycle appeared not to have seen me. He rode on without looking to right or left, straight out into the road.

Deirdre's car was not in front of the house so I assumed that she wasn't yet back, but as I came into the hall I saw her disappearing upstairs. She turned for a moment to see who had come in and said, 'Oh, it's you. I can't find Harvey anywhere and a man was looking for him about a mowing machine. And now the man's gone. Have you seen him? By the way, I've had a puncture.'

'How was the fair?' I asked.

'Ghastly,' she said, and then, as she continued her way upstairs, 'I bought those awful little pictures on the table there.'

I was struggling to get out of my wellington boots when I heard an upstairs door open and then Deirdre's harsh cry of 'Harvey!' pitched somewhere between surprise and admonition.

It may well be supposed at this point that what poor, unsuspecting, innocent Deirdre found was Harvey *in flagrante delicto* with Frances, but of course she was too late for that. What she found instead was the pair of them naked in her bed, steeped in post-coital slumber.

'There's a man here about a mower . . .' I heard her fatuously say, and then her voice trailed away as the telephone began to ring shrilly.

The next thing I knew was that she was calling my name. 'Will you come up here,' she demanded with sudden authority.

Numbly I obeyed her command, padding up the stairs with bare feet, for although I had at last pulled off my boots, I couldn't remember where I had left my shoes. As I reached Deirdre's side and looked through the door of the master bedroom, I saw Frances, slender and naked, snatching her clothes up off the floor. Harvey was still in bed and was talking on the telephone casually, almost as if nothing had happened.

Suddenly Frances – still unclothed – pushed past us both, a bundle of lingerie, lacy tights and a suede miniskirt under her arm.

'Too bad!' was all she said as she disappeared down the corridor towards her own room.

'There's a man downstairs still waiting to see you about a mower,' Deirdre repeated, presumably because at that juncture there didn't really seem to be very much else for her to say. 'Actually he may have gone,' she added, 'but you really ought to go and look for him.'

'That,' said Harvey, putting down the telephone, 'was the Valley Hospital—'

'The local bin,' Deirdre said in an aside to me by way of explanation. And to Harvey, 'What on earth did they want?'

'They've lost a patient,' said Harvey. 'A man. He's gone missing. He was seen in the village about an hour ago – he nicked a green bicycle from outside the post office and was seen heading in this direction. I think they're hoping to find him without having to contact the police.'

When Frances reappeared she was fully dressed in a pink trouser suit, wearing dark glasses with a mackintosh over one arm and an expensive-looking leather suitcase in her other hand. She came downstairs into the hall, dumped her bag and mackintosh by the front door and said to me – I happened to be hovering around, not quite knowing what to do with myself – 'I'm going back to London now.'

Quite how Frances went home or who took her to the station, I can't remember. There had been so much confusion, what with the man on the green bicycle and the puncture and then the Valley Hospital. The man, we heard later, wasn't picked up until the following day, having bicycled quite a distance and spent the night in a church porch, all miraculously without coming to any harm. Deirdre's flower paintings never reappeared.

I do remember thinking that I, too, ought to leave with Frances, but for some reason both Harvey and Deirdre persuaded me to stay. For one thing, they had asked some friends to supper and felt it would be easier if I was there. They also managed to persuade me that left to their own devices they might kill each other. In fact they begged me not to go, saying that what they both needed was a calm mediator. I was not feeling in the least bit calm and the last thing I wanted to do was to mediate between the pair of them, but perhaps what swayed me in the end was an awareness that Deirdre, who was looking so desperately unhappy, badly needed a friend. Harvey would be able to talk himself out of anything with a total disregard for his wife's or anyone else's feelings. He would steamroller over everyone and get his own way in the end – whatever his own way might turn out to be.

We didn't talk about what had happened that evening and the supper party passed off as if everything was normal, with Harvey his usual garrulous self, telling stories and making jokes and inventing – always inventing. The poor man on the green bicycle provided the basis for much of the conversation that evening, but little of what was said bore much relation to anything that had really happened. Harvey treated us to a few exotic theories of his own about mental illness.

It was at Sunday breakfast in the kitchen that, as far as I was concerned, the whole story really broke.

Deirdre appeared with red and swollen eyes and put the kettle on. She offered me fried eggs and bacon, which I would have refused except for the fact that she was doing them for herself. She needed them, she said.

She couldn't believe that she'd been so blind to what was

going on around her – the affair, Harvey had sworn to her, had only started that afternoon, but Deirdre had her doubts; she blamed herself, of course. She talked as she cooked the breakfast and then, just as she put the coffee on the table, Harvey appeared. He didn't look in the least little bit shamefaced.

In fact he announced that he couldn't help what had happened because he had fallen in love. I saw Deirdre wince.

'So what?' she asked tartly.

I vaguely wondered where George fitted into the picture.

'Oh, George – he doesn't really count.' Harvey waved a hand dismissively as if to push the thought of George out of the way. 'He's a cold fish, George – not a human being at all. In any case, he's been having an affair for years with a Romanian p-p-princess . . .'

Deirdre groaned as if to denote that she didn't want to hear any more lies.

After breakfast I walked with Harvey to the village to buy the Sunday newspapers. He told me then, swearing me to secrecy, that his affair with Frances had been going on for six months; it had started well before they all went to Italy. He was planning to leave Deirdre and to marry Frances. I could hardly believe it, his attitude seemed so casual, almost as if he were telling me he was going to buy a new car.

I wondered what on earth had made them all go on holiday together; I wondered about Deirdre and how she would fare and I wondered about Shackles and George again and about Frances's children.

Nothing seemed to trouble Harvey. He was used to getting what he wanted and he could see no reason why he should not do so now. Italy had been easy, was his only comment on that.

'You see,' he said, stopping in his tracks and turning

towards me, 'I regard love as a gift.' I can picture him now, head thrown back, arms flung out.

I said nothing but actually he was making me feel rather queasy.

Chapter IV

It was between marriages that Harvey became an art dealer. Certain he was, in those early days, of making a fortune, and, to tell the truth, he did initially do quite well. Beginner's luck, I suppose.

I hadn't been seeing much of him for a while when we bumped into each other by chance in the Fulham Road. Harvey was his usual ebullient self, apparently delighted to meet me, totally unaware – presumably quite unable to realize that everything which had happened before must perforce have left a shadow on our friendship. I'd watched him making Deirdre unhappy, which was one thing – their marriage was surely destined to failure from the start, besides which, once she was finally free and had eventually recovered from the break-up, Deirdre flourished. But I'd also watched him not minding in the slightest bit that he had hurt her, ruthlessly kicking her in the teeth, chucking her out like an old pair of shoes while banging on about love being a gift and all that sort of nonsense.

Funny kind of gift, I thought, which wreaks havoc, wrecks lives and allows those to whom it has been given ruthlessly to pursue their own advantage, grabbing what they can for themselves – heartless, heedless, simply not caring about the pain they inflict as they gallop like wild horses out of control towards a mirage.

Anyway, there he was – Harvey coming towards me, waving his arms, all hail-fellow-well-met. What ages it had been – must see more of each other – didn't even know where I was living now. Could we have lunch – dinner – must catch up – such a long time – best thing he ever did was to leave Shackles – get out of farming – been so much happier ever since – pictures – that was what he did now – must come and see his gallery . . .

We made a plan to meet the following week for lunch, although I still had reservations about how at ease I would ever be able to feel with Harvey now, but then we were very old friends and I had to accept that what had happened was all past history. Still, I found my mind turning back again and again to that awful weekend at Shackles and to the months which followed, when Deirdre was forever crying on my shoulder, when she finally cracked up and had to go to hospital, and even taciturn George rang me in desperation.

For a while Harvey and Frances had danced so narcissistic and so flamboyant a dance that all heads were turned, all eyes were on them and no one seemed able to talk of anything but their affair. Other couples have broken up without causing so much as a raised eyebrow, but there was something different about Harvey and Frances and about the way in which they went so blatantly for what they wanted, laughing as they did so, not stopping so much as to pay lip-service to anyone else's feelings. But at this distance it is impossible to remember what the ingredients exactly were which made this liaison so much more interesting than any other – which made people forget the time of day, world events, their own concerns. All because of their fascination with the seemingly unending saga of Harvey and Frances.

It may have been the heartlessness of the couple involved, or their belief that they existed outside the normal rules of society, that ultimately only they themselves counted, that their love was somehow sacred, that it had a unique quality, that they and only they had ever tasted the sweet fruits of passion, that they were different. It was at any rate all of this and more that temporarily destroyed Deirdre.

As I sat in the corner of the Italian restaurant where I had arranged to meet Harvey, smoking a little nervously and not in the least surprised that he was late for our lunch, my thoughts turned once more to the dramatic events of those days – dramatic events which in the light of new hopes and new anxieties seemed almost trivial as I looked back. I'd ordered a glass of sherry while I was waiting and was even contemplating ordering lunch when Harvey eventually appeared, unrepentant but full of excuses.

On the way to the restaurant – only a five-minute walk from his gallery – and I must come and see his gallery – he'd bumped into his ex-mother-in-law – frightfully embarrassing – dreadful woman – normally never left Lincolnshire – last person you'd expect to meet in the Fulham Road.

Then, of course, true to his old form, Harvey began to spin a yarn about Deirdre's mother who he claimed was an undischarged bankrupt and an alcoholic. None of her children would talk to her since their father had died two or three years before, but the thing was that in her downstairs lavatory – of all places – she had this amazing drawing which Harvey happened, between him and me, to know was worth a great deal of money. Harvey'd seen it. Harvey knew all about it and, if only he could get himself invited to the house in Lincolnshire, he'd be quids in.

I wondered if he was planning to steal the picture.

'You see,' he said, 'I met this man the other day . . .' He produced a ludicrous name, half Polish, half Italian, pronouncing it with a flourish as if it referred to someone very important about whom everyone ought to have heard. It meant nothing to me.

'One of those sorts of men,' he said, 'who sit all day in a lavatory halfway up the back stairs, sipping gin out of a bottle . . .' Didn't I know those kinds of men?

I couldn't immediately think of any men I knew who exactly fitted that category, but Harvey was away, in a world of his own.

'Always Gordons,' he added for verisimilitude. Anyway this particular character was a very well-known fellow in the art world – a dealer who'd twice made a million and lost it, who had an exceptional eye and, what was more to the point, who kept his ear to the ground.

Who kept his ear to the ground in a lavatory halfway up someone else's back stairs. 'Sounds like he's worth knowing,' I remarked tartly.

Anyway it turned out that this gin-sipping Slav had been invaluable to Harvey in setting up the gallery, had helped him to acquire a few good pictures which had got Harvey off to a fine start. I wondered what sort of a commission this character, whose first name was spelled with consonants only – all z's and c's – had taken, but Harvey is rather like the inveterate gambler who tells you the good news whilst forgetting the bad. He'll tell you that he's won five hundred pounds on the 2.30 but omit to inform you that he subsequently lost six hundred on the rest of the afternoon.

We were eating fresh pasta with clams and drinking some white wine which tasted of water, all of which suddenly made Harvey forget about his gallery for a moment in order to reminisce about Italy. He hadn't been back since he and Deirdre went there with Frances and George. They'd found one or two really good trattorias in Florence then, which led Harvey to the conclusion that in Italy there was no need to go for the more expensive restaurants. Italian food, according to Harvey, was a great deal better than French food, more innovative and more deeply rooted in the national character . . . So he went on.

In fact I was a little surprised at his referring to the notorious Italian holiday. No one thought that either he or Frances had come out of that episode particularly well. The whole performance had had a cynical but also slightly sadistic element – shades of laughter in the dark: Harvey and Frances bouncing about in bed, carefree, congratulating themselves on their deceit, laughing, while George sat in a bar reading Rilke or the instructions on a bottle of sun cream and Deirdre gazed at a mournful Cimabue.

As he talked, Harvey's mind raced ahead from the subject of food to women; where women were concerned, he preferred French ones to Italians. Harvey had never forgotten the first woman he slept with when he was only t-t-twelve years old – an exquisite creature and supremely intelligent, a young cousin of his mother's; it had all taken place in a château in the Tarn where his mother had taken him to learn French – well, he'd learned more than French – and to meet his French relations. Tante Marie-France – he'd seen her again since, years later, but she'd lost her looks – married to a collaborationist and wife-beater – had sought consolation with *le petit anglais*. And Tante Marie-France had had a few tricks up her sleeve.

Tante Marie-France must have been strange indeed to have turned to twelve-year-old Harvey for solace. But Harvey's earliest sexual encounters, about which he has been far more informative – or misinformative – than anyone else I have ever met, will, surely, be forever shrouded in mystery, which is just as it should be. I might add, though, that they or their ghosts at least have been ever present, perpetually lurking off stage, waiting to be called upon by Harvey's wingéd fantasy whenever he, driven by the inner workings of his own peculiar psyche, has needed to reassure himself of his own supremacy.

Having dealt with the subject of Tante Marie-France and having, as he no doubt thought, presented himself as a precocious Lothario, presumably thus to re-establish his credibility which he may have felt slipping as he mentioned the Florentine holiday, Harvey suddenly went back to talking about his business.

What he really wanted to do was to get this foreign-sounding friend of his with a gin bottle to go up to Lincolnshire with him to call on Deirdre's mother. It had been quite lucky as a matter of fact, bumping into the old girl just now. He'd been able to chat her up a bit – prepare the ground. The trouble was that she'd never really liked him, but then there was no reason for her to feel so strongly now that he was no longer married to her daughter. He had a hunch that she'd in fact been quite pleased to see him. He wanted to get that man into her downstairs lavatory to have a look at her drawing.

I remarked that from what I'd heard, there wouldn't be much difficulty in getting Harvey's friend into the lavatory.

Harvey wasn't listening, or he just didn't want to hear any facetious jokes. He was in deadly earnest.

After lunch we walked round the corner to see the gallery. A discreet shop front presented itself as the only business premises in a narrow residential street of white-stuccoed terraced houses. Harvey Hotham's name was painted in unobtrusive italics – no capitals – over the window, in which was displayed, against a dark backcloth, a small quasi-naive painting of a boat tossing about on a choppy sea.

'Cornish painter,' Harvey said, waving a hand vaguely in the direction of the window as he pushed the shop door, which tinkled as it opened. The floor of the gallery was thickly carpeted in purple Wilton and the white walls were sparsely dotted with pictures, most of them in the same style as the one in the window, of more or less exceptional quality. Sideways to a reproduction Sheraton sofa table set at an angle across the corner of the room sat a lissom young woman dressed in a puce velvet jacket and maroon crushed-velvet trousers. Her long legs stretched almost interminably across the floor of the shop and her long, blond, untidy hair practically hid her face. She was smoking a cigarette.

'This is Melissa – my assistant.' Harvey waved a hand in Melissa's direction in much the same way as he had waved at the picture in the window.

'Have some brandy.' He dived towards a small Regency chiffonier which stood discreetly at the further end of the gallery, the only piece of furniture apart from Melissa's table and a couple of chairs, and brought out two glasses and a bottle of Rémy Martin. I noticed he didn't offer any brandy to Melissa.

I remember it was a very hot day – it must have been June or July, I think – and the smoke from Melissa's cigarette hung heavily in the room and lingered in the air, somewhat interfering with the viewing of the pictures.

Harvey was quite excited, seeming suddenly to show off in front of the languid Melissa. I wondered what his relationship with her was and decided that it probably didn't exist beyond what one saw except in the interstices of Harvey's mind –

perhaps not even there yet. He was certainly very preoccupied with his venture and all the Cornish paintings which his Italo-Polish friend had put him in the way of.

'Wonderful!' he told me. He was just about to catch a boom.

Melissa, who hadn't yet spoken except to mouth a greeting as we came in, stubbed out her cigarette, immediately lit another, inhaled deeply and blew the smoke out of her mouth slowly and with concentration. She looked sullen and for a brief moment reminded me of Frances.

I didn't really want to drink brandy on that hot afternoon so after I'd taken a couple of sips and looked at the few pictures, I left, promising to keep in touch with Harvey and wishing him well.

As I shut the door of the shop, I glanced back over my shoulder and saw Harvey perch precariously and I would have thought foolishly on the edge of the sofa table, arms folded across his chest, and bend as if to speak intimately to Melissa, who, without turning to look at him, merely drew concentratedly on her cigarette and exhaled slowly again.

Despite our protestations of undying friendship, I didn't see Harvey for quite some time after that, although I did eventually hear what happened to Deirdre's mother's drawing.

Harvey, who is nothing if not brazen, formed a plan whereby he and his mentor – let's call him Zed – would happen to find themselves in Lincolnshire, not far from where she lived, and would invite themselves to call. This in itself seemed pretty daft to me since Mrs Drew can hardly have delighted in the prospect of entertaining someone who had made her daughter so unhappy. It wasn't true to say, as Harvey had, that Mrs Drew never liked him from the start. At first she'd been thrilled to bits with a marriage which took her last daughter off her hands and freed her to sell the

London flat and go back home to Lincolnshire. Besides, Harvey was well off and, as she initially thought, full of charm. But by the time of the divorce, she made no secret at all of her feelings for her reprobate son-in-law. Indeed, there was no crime of which she would not willingly have believed him to be guilty.

In any case Harvey and Zed set out from London in Zed's ten-year-old Jaguar which, due to a series of financial misfortunes, Zed had not seen fit to keep serviced. But, he asserted, 'Jaguar is perfectly made car – like perfectly made woman she keep going.'

Harvey thought Zed was frightfully funny. That was until the perfectly made car broke down outside Leicester.

After a considerable amount of hassle, the Jaguar was eventually towed away to a garage where a mechanic scratched the back of his head and declared, when asked for a prognosis, that he couldn't rightly say, he'd have to take a look at the car first, and, no, he wouldn't be able to do it that afternoon. Very busy time of year, they had a lot of work on – wouldn't care to say whether the problem was likely to be serious or not. Could be just a small thing – could take only a couple of hours to fix and then again, it could be something quite major – couldn't tell till he'd looked at it. He went on scratching his head. Then again it depended on the parts – been having trouble getting parts lately . . . And so he went on.

Harvey and Zed ended up staying the night in the last room they could find in a grim hotel in Leicester, side by side in twin beds, sleeping in raspberry-coloured nylon sheets. It was before the days when the influence of *nouvelle cuisine* spread even to the provinces, so that they had to put up not only with slimy sheets but with thick gravy poured in a custardlike coating over grey meat, which might have been anything but for the presence of mint and redcurrant jelly which proclaimed it to be lamb. Solid lumps of mashed potato were served from ice-cream scoops and the copious vegetables were tasteless and watery. When the ice cream came, it was indistinguishable in appearance from the mashed potatoes.

By the morning Harvey was feeling restless and irritable; he couldn't wait to go to the garage and to be on the road again – get out of Leicester. A provincial hotel in the Midlands was hardly the kind of place in which he was pleased to hang about. Zed, on the other hand, was apparently as happy as a cricket, wonderfully amused by everything around him, not the least bit perturbed by the grey meat or the nylon sheets. He had a bottle of gin in his overnight bag and, according to Harvey, would happily have spent the rest of the day sitting in the lounge of that dingy hotel, sipping surreptitiously from the bottle. Perhaps he was in no hurry to hear the worst about his car – perhaps he was in no hurry in life. He was certainly the kind of person who – so long as someone else was picking up the tab – would gladly hang around in bars or hotels until eternity. It could even have crossed his mind that Harvey might pick up the tab at the garage.

However it may have been, Harvey had certainly begun to find Zed less hilariously funny than he had done formerly. The flat back of Zed's head with its closely cut grey hair and sticking-out ears was beginning to get on Harvey's nerves – and why the hell couldn't the fellow stop smiling? He kept on smiling in that hotel, sitting there clasping his bottle of gin and making inane quasi-philosophical remarks about life and death and freedom and then suddenly bursting into manic laughter at the thought of the human condition and of all the people in Leicester and the broken Jaguar and the incongruity of the two of them just being there together.

Eventually Harvey managed to inject a hint of a sense of urgency into Zed – or at least to cause him to realize that he, Harvey, felt the need to be doing something. After all, they were in this thing together, they both knew what they had come for and they must get on.

Harvey had sent Mrs Drew a postcard from London announcing that he would be in Lincolnshire on business and hoping that he might have the pleasure of looking in to see her. I can imagine that he was all keyed up and didn't want to bungle the plan or in any way to put Mrs Drew's back up. Funny that he'd never thought of that before, when he was married to Deirdre. In those days he'd have done anything to avoid having to visit his parents-in-law, making no secret of the fact that he found them terrifically dull. On the rare occasions that he did go to Lincolnshire, or see them in the south, he made no attempt whatsoever to ingratiate himself with them.

I remember being at Shackles once with Deirdre's parents and being appalled by quite how offhand Harvey was to them – to the point of walking out of the room when his mother-in-law came in, or picking up a newspaper when his father-in-law began to reminisce about Burma where he'd been years ago, back in the twenties before he was ever married. Burma was an ever-recurring theme with Deirdre's father – perhaps he felt that it represented the freedom he seemed to have lost for ever with his marriage.

If his father-in-law had still been alive, Harvey might never have set off so confidently with Zed in search of the drawing in his downstairs lavatory. Harvey, being Harvey, most likely thought that a woman was an easy touch and that he, with his masculine charm and a few compliments of the 'a-pretty-woman-like-you' variety, would have no problem getting round Mrs Drew, which, on this occasion, unfortunately proved to be more or less right.

Mrs Drew was not, as Harvey so confidently asserted, an undischarged bankrupt, but when her husband died he was found to have left his affairs in some kind of disarray which condemned his widow to severely straitened circumstances. Had he intended to punish her for all his years of lost freedom, he could hardly have done so more successfully. The poor woman who had throughout her life assiduously avoided having anything to do with business or money, found herself wandering, lost in a wilderness of debt and incertitude.

Whether or not the wretched woman was, as Harvey also claimed, an alcoholic, must remain a matter for conjecture, for although I have occasionally heard Deirdre, with a weary sigh, announce that her mother drinks too much – how much too much I do not know. Whatever else she was, or was not, one can reasonably presume Mrs Drew to have been a lonely, anxious widow at that stage.

Of course Harvey claimed that she was 'pie-eyed' by the time he turned up with Zed. I don't suppose Zed was especially sober, either.

Zed's car had been declared unroadworthy, being in need of a new clutch, new brake shoes and a new gearbox, not to mention four new tyres, none of which things this two-times millionaire could begin to afford, so that he was obliged to abandon it in Leicester in the hope that some dupe might be persuaded to buy its poor, ailing carcass from the garage. Harvey made no offer to bale Zed out and was merely intensely irritated at having so great an inconvenience foisted on him on this important trip. They were obliged to hire a car for the continuation of their journey and travelled on, one might imagine, in stony silence – except for the fact that neither Harvey nor Zed would have been able to stop talking for very long.

They reached Stamford in the late afternoon, booked into the George Hotel, settled into their comfortable rooms – no nylon sheets here – and then Harvey went to telephone Mrs Drew. Judging by the enthusiasm with which she greeted Harvey's arrival in the north, she must have been a lonely woman indeed. Normally she would have had very little to say to him – let alone to Zed.

Mrs Drew lived in a bleak old red brick rectory which stood between a group of elms and a church whose tall, pointed spire could be seen across the wold from a distance of many miles. Beneath the wide sky the hamlet seemed to be perched on the edge of a world from whence it might at any moment be blown away by the whistling east winds that swept in over the North Sea from Siberia and the Urals. The house had seen better days and had dilapidated rapidly during the two or three years since Cecil Drew's death.

With her shaky finances firmly controlled by the grasping hands of solicitors, Mrs Drew lived like a church mouse, repairing nothing, never turning on the heating but squatting by the Aga when alone or, if visitors came, warming a room at a time with one bar of an electric fire. But visitors were few and far between and the gardener she had sacked, thus abandoning her one-time beautiful flower beds to be swamped by bindweed and couch grass. Roses struggled with brambles for survival as ground elder stifled the herbaceous border. In the vegetable garden the asparagus bed had disappeared, dandelions and docks rampaged where once there had been orderly rows of carrots or beans, and panes of glass had been blown off the roof of the greenhouse, leaving it no longer usable. There was nothing Mrs Drew could do to contain this decline since she herself was quite severely smitten with arthritis and could barely hold a trowel, let alone a garden fork, in her crippled hands.

Not unlike Deirdre before her metamorphosis, Mrs Drew was a pale, colourless woman whose self-image was so negative that she had never even learned to flirt. Her hair, like Deirdre's when she married Harvey, was scraped back into a tight, prim knot. It was thin and grey and her face perpetually wore the expression of one who is sad but long-suffering and who expects nothing more from a life which has already proved to be disappointing. At times it seemed that her expression was almost more apologetic than long-suffering.

She certainly was an apologetic woman, self-effacing and more than usually humbled by her penniless circumstances. Before she was widowed she at least felt that she had some status as Cecil's wife, for Cecil was a busy member of the community, a magistrate, chairman of the local golf club and so on. But now she was nothing. Sometime mother and wife.

As soon as Harvey and Zed arrived she began to apologize – for the weather, the wind, the overgrown garden. 'Of course Harvey can remember it all in Cecil's day.' She addressed Zed and her hands trembled as she poured a small glass of dark sherry.

Zed noticed narrow hands which must have been pretty before the arthritis took a hold. He glanced at her face, which he then noticed was pretty too, if you looked carefully. Fine bones.

'I'm afraid we can't afford a gardener any more so the garden's gone quite to pieces. I'm so sorry that you should see it like this.' Then she wanted to know what had brought the two of them to Lincolnshire and to apologize again for being so dull and for not having company.

Harvey explained that they had come to see a man about a

very important picture and then, for fear of being asked for further details, he launched into talking about his business. He chatted away as though Mrs Drew were his oldest and best friend, telling her what he wanted her to know which, as he represented it, was that he was now a highly successful, much respected and knowledgeable art dealer. He did not mention the drawing in the lavatory but instead remarked that, having met her so recently by chance in London, he felt that it would hardly have been civil to come to the neighbourhood without looking her up. It was truly a pleasure for him to be back in the old house again, the garden looked as lovely as ever and Deirdre – how was Deirdre? He was so glad that things had turned out well for Deirdre. The fact that they had must, I suppose, have alleviated his guilt, if he had any. But then again, perhaps he hadn't, for who was he to go asking after Deirdre?

In days gone by he had used to say that the one person he felt badly about was George, but everyone took that with a pinch of salt.

At a certain point Zed, who had been quietly eyeing the contents of the room while sipping his thimbleful of sherry and longing for a snifter of something stronger, rose to his feet and asked where the toilet was. Mrs Drew, having apologized of course for not having told him earlier, led him out of the room and pointed down a cold corridor.

At this moment, Harvey admits, he began to feel excited. He hoped Zed wouldn't make a mess of things – wouldn't put his foot in it. Perhaps the picture had been hung elsewhere. What would they do then? Or perhaps it had already been sold. Cecil Drew always used to say that it was too good to be in the lavatory and that it ought to be moved. It was, or so Cecil's mother from whom it came had always led him to believe, by Canaletto – a view across the Thames.

Nothing very special in Cecil's view, but then – if it was a Canaletto – perhaps it deserved better treatment.

If Zed decided it probably was a Canaletto, Harvey was sure he would soon be able to persuade Mrs Drew to part with it. He could see how she had fallen on hard times and would welcome the cash. Unattributed, it naturally wouldn't fetch her that much money, but she would obviously be glad of something. Once the attribution was ascertained, Harvey would be able to sell it on for a bomb and make himself a tidy little profit. If Zed was wrong and the drawing could not be attributed, then nothing much would have been lost. Harvey was sure that he'd be able to sell it quite easily in any case. It was a pretty thing.

Never at any stage has Harvey been able to comprehend the dicey ethics involved in such a strategy. As far as he could see – and I feel sure that he would say the same today – he would be doing his ex-mother-in-law a good turn just at a time when she most needed it. His job was to deal in pictures; he had to make a living somehow and, without his interference, she would never have sold the drawing anyway.

I sometimes wonder if Harvey should be entirely blamed for the tricky paths he has trodden through life, weaving forever this way and that to his own advantage, apparently innately incapable of seeing things from anyone else's point of view, incapable of feeling for another person. Was it the early adulation of a doting mother that helped to blind him to anything but his own version of the truth? Did he consciously and intentionally at some stage close one part of his mind to unwanted information in order to protect himself against life's vicissitudes? Certainly there exists some obfuscation to prevent his intelligence from ever willingly contemplating reality.

It seemed to Harvey that Zed was spending an awfully

long time in the lavatory and the tension of waiting merely encouraged him to talk. By the time Zed eventually reappeared, Harvey was banging on about the history of the water closet, which he claimed had been invented by the Egyptians nearly three thousand years before Christ during the Early Dynastic period. The positioning of the water closet had been determined by the relationship of the stars to one another during certain months of the year . . . Harvey was stuttering a little.

Mrs Drew's back was turned to the room; with trembling hand she was refilling her glass with brown sherry. Harvey was sitting in a shabby armchair covered in faded cretonne, arms waving, legs outstretched, talking as it were to the winds. Zed's instructions were that on returning from the lavatory he should scratch his head if he thought the drawing was worth having. If he genuinely thought that there was a coup to be brought off.

In fact what happened was that when Zed returned, he was so surprised by the sight of Harvey sprawling in the chair and the sound of him laying down the law about ancient Egyptian water closets, that he instantly forgot whether or not he was supposed to be scratching his head. He couldn't for the life of him remember what a scratch would signify, so for a moment he stood hesitating in the doorway, wondering what to do, when, all of a sudden, he had an appalling itch on top of his head which he naturally felt an almost irresistible urge to scratch. In order to restrain himself from scratching he began to twist and turn awkwardly like a child needing hurriedly to return to the lavatory whence he had just come.

Harvey, halted in mid-sentence, stared in amazement at his gyrating friend: short, bandy legs, worn shapeless jeans.

Mrs Drew, having refilled her glass, was walking slowly and carefully, eyes fixed in concentration on the brimming sherry, back across the room towards the sofa where she had been sitting, apparently oblivious to the machinations of the other two.

Suddenly Zed could stand the itch on his head no longer and with frantic, jerky movements began scratching, saying meanwhile as a means of explaining to Harvey that the action was quite unconnected to any agreement they had made earlier, 'My head, he tickles.'

Not surprisingly, Harvey failed completely to take the hint but instead immediately imagined that his fortune had been made.

Mrs Drew, having successfully negotiated her passage across the room, was, by this time, back on the sofa, carefully sipping sherry, perhaps even beginning to wonder what these two clowns were up to.

'We're hoping to be able to get a little help in the garden next year,' she ventured.

Harvey was sitting there with his mouth hanging open, dollar signs no doubt swimming in front of his eyes. Zed was still scratching his head and twisting awkwardly in the doorway. Neither he nor Harvey was remotely interested in Mrs Drew's garden, although it did at some moment cross Harvey's mind to wonder why she repeatedly used the personal pronoun in the first person plural when she talked about it or about anything else for that matter. Was it habit, self-deluding comfort or was there really someone else lurking in the background with the power to prevent Harvey's dreamed-of deal? Deirdre and her sisters?

'This one – ' Zed with sudden urgency pointed at a dark corner of the sitting room, revealing holes under the arms of his baggy jersey as he did so – 'this one is fine picture.' He began to scratch even more violently than before.

Both Harvey and Mrs Drew turned to look at a small,

rather dirty landscape painting of some very English fields with trees and swirling clouds through which, despite the grime of years, the light broke in bursts of intermittent radiance.

'Ah, yes.' Mrs Drew had at last deposited her glass on an occasional table by the sofa. 'That one – we have always been very fond of that one. We bought it for nothing years ago in a little junk shop there was in Stamford. Went out of business a long time ago now . . . I always used to tell Cecil that if we ever fell on hard times, it might save our bacon and turn out to be a Constable.' She laughed a surprisingly bitter laugh. 'We should be so lucky!'

'Constable I don't think.' Zed was trying to collect himself as he stepped towards the picture to look at it more closely, still scratching desperately as he did so. 'But nice picture.' He looked at Harvey, trying to catch his eye, and continued to scratch.

Chapter V

I have often asked myself what exactly it is about Harvey that not only makes his friends continue to be fond of him, but also makes him a subject of such absorbing interest to us all. There is hardly one of us that he has not betrayed at some time to a greater or lesser degree, and yet we have come back for more. We have forgiven and for the most part forgotten. Whenever two or three of us have gathered together barely half an hour has elapsed before someone has asked after Harvey. Then we have all smiled, sighed or shrugged our shoulders and out has come an account of his latest exploits. Only the recently wounded still rattle a sabre.

Even Deirdre has at times been able to laugh kindly and say, 'Poor old Harvey', although I have to say it was a while before she was able to be so detached. I think she decided at some stage that there was an element missing in his make-up which means he is of diminished responsibility. Perhaps to think of it like this not only helps to explain his treatment of her but may, too, at some stage, have made it less painful for her. Whatever the case, she certainly soon learned that she was better off without him and that their marriage was a mistake on both their parts. Sometimes, even now, when he is mentioned, a faraway look will come into her eyes and a quietness will overcome her, and then I wonder what she's thinking. Whether she really can still have a residual soft spot for him or whether she is just one of those people for whom the past is unbearably poignant.

Certainly the last months spent at Shackles were times of such unhappiness that Deirdre can hardly wish to look back on them very often. Harvey was prancing about the place, glowing with the thrill of his love affair, talking to everyone he met about how wonderful it was to be in love, how he had never felt like this about anyone before, how Frances and he had this magical 'rapport' which lifted his behaviour out of the ordinary, set some holy seal on it and made everything permissible.

Frances was nearly as bad except that she talked less, but merely wallowed in her own beauty, in adulation and in the notoriety of it all.

Deirdre begged Harvey to make up his mind about what he was going to do. Did he intend to leave her? In which case, the sooner they parted the better – or would he give Frances up and try to make the marriage work?

From the outside, it was perfectly clear that Harvey was so high on the drug of eroticism that he would be totally incapable of giving Frances up. Most people also thought that the best thing Deirdre could possibly do for her own good would be to boot him out. Let him get on with it. He would tire eventually of Frances – or she of him – and before long he would be looking around for someone new to enchant him, someone else to seduce, to parade in front of, and where would that leave Deirdre?

And what of Frances? The big question was, would she leave George or not? How much more could George tolerate?

In those days I was constantly in touch with Deirdre, who – perhaps because I had been at Shackles on that fateful weekend – used my shoulder to cry on. I had no idea of how to help her or of what to advise her to do. In any case my advice or anyone else's for that matter would have been irrelevant since she had ultimately either to choose her own path with regard to Harvey or to plan for a future life without him. Nothing of what she was saying at the time was particularly constructive, no doubt because she was so bitterly unhappy. Harvey had told her that it was all her fault their relationship had failed, that in the past he had needed her but he no longer did. She could stay at Shackles for the time being if she wanted, as he hadn't decided what he was going to do.

Of course what he would do in the end appeared to depend entirely on Frances, whom, we soon realized, Harvey was trying to prise away from George. Yet there was something about the relationship between George and Frances which made most people doubt that Harvey would in the end succeed in breaking up their marriage. Frances had always treated George in a fairly high-handed way, but it appeared, from the outside at any rate, that George was generally prepared to cast a blind eye on his wife's infidelities and that there existed between the two of them some intangible thread of steel which it would be extremely difficult to break. I think most people thought that in the end Frances would tire of Harvey and return to George and to whatever modicum of domesticity she might be prepared to tolerate until she was ready for the next fling. After all it was perfectly apparent to everyone else, so it must have been apparent to her too, that Harvey was a lightweight compared to the far more substantial George.

How well I remember the day that Deirdre finally rang me to say that that was it: Harvey and Frances had gone away together. It was all over. In her heart she knew that it could never really have worked with her and Harvey but all the same she felt she had reached the end of the road. She was a totally useless person, incapable of making sense of her life, unequipped to earn a living, incapable of anything, unable even to bear children.

That was the first I had ever heard mention of that. I had no idea how I could possibly console her – nothing I could think of to say seemed remotely appropriate and in any case I doubt she would have heard since she was sobbing and crying, talking incoherently, blaming Frances, blaming herself, blaming Harvey, repeating herself, contradicting herself, in fact – temporarily, as it turned out – utterly destroyed. She begged me to come down to Shackles to be with her. She was there alone with her little dog, and, fearful of what she might do, I decided to go.

During the preceding months Deirdre had been tormented by Harvey's – and indeed Frances's – lack of consideration for her, so that when the final break came it could have been hoped that she might see it as a move forward and might even feel a sense of relief. Frances, she told me, had during that time bombarded the house with endless letters to Harvey, which he, on his rare visits home, would cheerfully read in front of Deirdre before throwing them casually to one side and leaving them around for anyone to see. Deirdre, between tears, was able to laugh bitterly at a few maudlin or pretentiously poetical sentences from Frances's hand which she had committed to memory. There was a peculiar phrase concerning the beauty of Harvey's elongated, rather bumpy feet resembling the dark hands of an Arab on an alien shore, sensitive and tortured. Deirdre thought Harvey's feet were hideous. Other people's love letters, we agreed, rarely did credit to the writer.

So Frances had left George and Harvey had finally left Deirdre and the pair of them had – as they say – run away together and the gossips were full of it. Misinformation of every kind was in the ascendant.

Harvey, without a murmur, immediately put Shackles on the market, told Deirdre that he couldn't help it because he was so in love. In love – so in love, which of course meant that he could do exactly as he pleased – indeed that he could fly.

And fly they did. Before Deirdre could so much as bat an eyelid or wipe away a single tear, Harvey and Frances had flown away – no one knew where. That was when Deirdre rang me.

It was several days before George was able to tell Deirdre that he had heard from Frances in New York, where she and Harvey had apparently gone to get away from it all. At the same time Knight, Frank and Rutley were forever sending people to view Shackles, expecting poor Deirdre to show them round not only the house, but the farm as well.

During the few days I spent at Shackles with Deirdre, I tried to persuade her quite simply to refuse to have anything to do with the sale until Harvey came back from America. She sometimes managed to convince herself that when he came back, it would be for good, and that if she helped him to sell the house and farm, then they could start again somewhere else and everything would be all right. She seemed unable to cope with the ultimate humiliation of being unwanted.

As I have said, it seemed quite clear to the rest of us that Harvey would never return to a marriage that had obviously never even got off the ground, and what indeed would have been the point for either partner? But none of that made the moment any easier for Deirdre and anyway who was I to point it out?

The waters were further muddied by telephone calls from George, who, although much more laid back than Deirdre could ever have known how to be, was, by all accounts, devastated. He could generally tolerate Frances's infidelity because he loved her and because he firmly believed that it never really meant very much. She was like that: she needed the diversion. He and Frances were both tricky people but he was convinced that they had a unique understanding of each other and an absolute need of one another, that they had an extraordinary emotional and intellectual bond which transcended mere sexual infidelity. Their children hardly seemed to enter the equation at all.

It was strange to hear that George had said so much, or spoken so freely to anyone about his marriage. It was also rather disturbing because it made Deirdre think that Frances was about to go back to George, which would mean Harvey returning to her. And so she went on hoping – and crying.

In New York Harvey and Frances were staying at the Algonquin Hotel, lying about in bed, ordering bull shots and pecan pie from room service, running up enormous bills which Harvey presumably imagined would be covered by the sale of Shackles. When they came back they told everyone that they had had a wonderful time – perfectly blissful. It had been just what they needed. They were happy and refreshed. The rest of the world could clearly go hang.

My visit to Shackles then was unbearably fraught, with Deirdre so very much at a loss as to what to do. Unable in fact to act at all, unable to make any decisions. I warned her that I could not stay for long – I had to get back to London, yet I was loath to leave her alone in her present state of mind. She had entirely lost her appetite but was drinking quite a lot; she had sleeping pills from her doctor but assured me that she still lay awake half the night or at least woke in the small hours, never to go back to sleep. When she was not crying or talking away tensely, overexcited and irrational, she would sit speechless – almost lifeless – for hours on end, unusually for her smoking a good deal, with her little dog on her lap.

Eventually I gave up trying to get her to decide on anything; it was pointless since she couldn't even decide on what we should have for lunch. I did a bit of shopping and elementary cooking and looked after her as best I could. I kept her company and tried to think of who could come and be with her when I left. She rejected the idea of either of her sisters on the grounds that they had families which they would be unable to leave. Her mother, she was convinced, would not be able to abandon her father and as for a variety of other friends, they had either jobs or babies and in any case she wouldn't want to ask them. She would be all right, she assured me.

Desperate to know what to do and terrified of leaving Deirdre alone, I finally decided to ring one of her sisters without telling her. I had met Marion once a few years before but had no idea whether she would remember me or indeed have any idea who I was, but I thought it worth a try.

Marion is a tall, matter-of-fact woman with the heavy good looks of her father, unlike Deirdre who inherited their mother's slight build. At the time she lived near Salisbury. Although all our friends knew and had known for some time what had been going on with Harvey and Deirdre, nothing about it had reached Deirdre's family. The second sister lived in the north of England and none of the three saw each other at all regularly, besides which Deirdre and Harvey moved in quite different circles to the rest of the Drew family.

So Marion was not only appalled by what I had to tell her, but taken totally by surprise. Being a practical woman, she immediately began to make suggestions as to what Deirdre ought to be doing. She should see a solicitor without delay, refuse to leave the marital home, keep the house well locked up to prevent Harvey from sneaking back unexpectedly and helping himself to any of the furniture or effects.

It was clear that Marion quite failed to understand the burden of my song; she had no grasp at all of what I was trying to tell her about her sister. Consequently I felt rather foolish standing there in the village telephone box, talking to this virtual stranger about her sister, with my money about to run out. I tried to interrupt the flow of efficiency coming from the other end of the line.

'Deirdre,' I said, 'is not well – she—'

But Marion was still going on about solicitors and the wife's rights when my money ran out and the telephone went dead with her still talking at the other end. I really didn't know what to do. I could hardly ring the other sister, whom I'd certainly never met and whose name I didn't even know. I would have to try Marion again, I decided, but first of all I would have to get some more coins for the call box.

I walked up to the village shop, where they obliged me with change for a pound, and then went back to the telephone only to discover that Marion's number was engaged. I waited five minutes before dialling it again, to find it was still engaged.

Really I suppose I had acted rather clumsily. As I walked back through the front door of Shackles, I could hear Deirdre talking on the telephone in the sitting room but I couldn't hear what she was saying and of course had no idea to whom she might be talking. I just put my head round the door to give her the cigarettes I had bought for her at the village shop and was turning to go away again when I heard her say, 'No, Marion, there is nothing you can do . . .' And then she burst into tears.

I left the room then but was aware that the conversation continued for some time, with Marion, no doubt, offering a lot of practical but, under the circumstances, quite impractical advice, probably telling Deirdre to stop crying and to try to pull herself together.

But in the end even Marion, with her limited understanding, was able to grasp that Deirdre was in no position to pull herself together and so, to my intense relief, she decided to come and take charge the following day. She could farm her children out for the night, prepare a meal for her husband which she would leave in the fridge with instructions about how to heat it up and what order to eat it in, and be at Shackles by early afternoon. She intended, I think, to stay one night and then to persuade Deirdre to go home with her, where she was welcome to stay until Harvey reappeared to take some responsibility for his actions.

I was glad to think that I would be able to leave for London with a quiet conscience. Deirdre was in a bad way but it was certainly beyond my powers to help her. I cursed Harvey in my mind as I lay awake that night, for ever having married her, and wondered what on earth was going to happen to her now. For her part, Deirdre seemed to sense that it was pointless to put up any further resistance to Marion, although she certainly didn't relish the prospect of her arrival and had no desire whatsoever to go back to Salisbury with her.

When Marion eventually arrived, she jumped out of a large Rover, released two black Labradors from a cage at the back and strode purposefully up to the front door, her hounds at her heels.

'I knew you wouldn't mind the dogs,' she said to Deirdre as the two black monsters cowered round her ankles, tails between their legs, snarling lips curled, terrified of the cheerful little terrier which ran yapping towards them. 'I couldn't leave them behind,' she explained, 'because Nick would probably have forgotten to feed them.' Marion is one of those women whose confidence in her own ability to cope, to organize, to remember and to do, extends to a belief that everyone else is completely incompetent. As she shook my hand with her firm, masculine grasp, she gave me a cursory glance as much as to imply that I, too, was one of the world's incompetents. She looked at me as one might look at someone else's child crying in a shop, with a mixture of irritation at its having impinged at all and relief that it is not one's responsibility. Then she turned away and addressed herself to her sister. Deirdre immediately began to cry. I went upstairs to pack my bags, deeming it suitable that I should leave the sisters alone together as soon as possible.

Before I left we had a quick cup of tea in the kitchen, Marion having already taken complete control. Accepted at last by the Cairn, her dogs lay somnolent under the table while she moved efficiently and confidently around the kitchen, apparently as familiar with it as if it were her own – large, handsome face in repose, large, competent hands warming a teapot, wiping the draining board, spooning leaves into the teapot, putting cups on the table, milk in a jug, teaspoons, sugar – all so neat, all so ordered, as if this minor order could influence poor weeping Deirdre and impose order on her troubled mind. To me she hardly spoke, seeing me, I suppose, as some sort of intruder and certainly wondering what I came to be doing there.

On leaving, I put an arm round Deirdre, begged her to try to be brave, assured her that she could call on me any time and promised to contact her within a few days. She hardly responded at all and seemed to have collapsed completely. Marion, I think, imagined that it was my presence that inhibited her sister and consequently must have longed for me to be out of the house.

That was the last time I ever went to Shackles – where we had all been used to having such fun.

That night Deirdre retired early to bed. She had, it appears, been quite calm throughout the evening. No tears. Marion was certain that she had arrived at just the right moment. All Deirdre needed was a few days' rest – after all, she had suffered a shock – and then, having taken stock of what had happened, she would be feeling quite well enough to plan her future. She would go to a solicitor, sort out her affairs, decide where she wanted to live, start to look for somewhere – a small flat in London would suit her admirably – and then, of course, she could start looking for a job. Hadn't she learned to type at some stage? There should be no problem. In fact the only problem was the dog. Since the Labradors had calmed down, Marion suggested that she might even consider taking the terrier home with her and adopting it.

Deirdre, it appears, spoke little throughout the evening, but Marion was greatly relieved by her acquiescence. She agreed to go back to Salisbury for a day or two, she agreed to go to a solicitor, to begin looking for a flat, she agreed to Marion adopting her dog – quite calmly she agreed to it all. Then she kissed her sister, thanked her for coming, said that it really hadn't been necessary, apologized for being a nuisance and went to bed.

The following morning Marion was back in the kitchen by

eight o'clock, as confident as ever. Deirdre, she decided, could do with the rest, she could sleep in for a while. In fact Marion, as she prepared toast and coffee, was congratulating herself on how well she had organized everything. Deirdre was clearly relieved by the arrangements and so had had a good night's sleep, otherwise she would have already been down in the kitchen – or at least Marion would have heard her moving about upstairs.

At nine o'clock Patsy, the daily help, arrived. Marion introduced herself and explained that Deirdre was having a lie-in. She would be down shortly. If not, Marion would have to wake her, as she intended to be back home by lunchtime. Patsy, on her way to fetch the hoover, tripped over the tail of one of the Labradors. It turned and snarled at her.

'He wouldn't harm a fly,' said Marion. 'He's an old softie – aren't you, Nero?' The thing about Marion, Marion explained to Patsy, was that she preferred animals to human beings. They were so much nicer in every way because they never did the dreadful things that humans were always doing. And they were far more sensible – didn't allow themselves to get worked up about things, didn't talk a lot of nonsense.

'They certainly don't do that,' said Patsy with a sideways look at Marion and a snarl almost as intimidating as Nero's.

By half past nine Marion was beginning to grow somewhat impatient. She kept looking at her watch and tapping it with the index finger of her right hand. She had eaten her own breakfast long ago and cleared it up, she had packed her overnight bag and put it in the Rover along with the rugs she had brought for the dogs to sleep on. The toast she had made for Deirdre was growing hard and dry in the rack.

Patsy, who was washing the floor, thought it odd that Deirdre hadn't come down yet; she was usually up and about, if only in her dressing gown, by the time Patsy arrived, generally complaining of being unable to sleep. Perhaps Marion ought to go and see if she was all right.

No one really knows to this day – even she herself is unsure – whether or not Deirdre really meant to take her own life. When Marion found her she was in a deep, apparently undisturbable sleep. Marion of course did not panic but immediately called 999 for an ambulance, shouted for Patsy to help and, picking her sister up out of bed, began to drag her around the room, talking coaxingly as she did so. Telling her, I wouldn't be surprised, that she had been a silly old thing. Somewhere Marion had read that it was important, under such circumstances, to keep the drugged person on the move, keep them awake at all costs, march them up and down if possible, however much they kept trying to sleep.

From time to time Deirdre, propped up between her sister and Patsy, head lolling, emitted a groan and her eyelids began to flicker, which convinced Marion that she was almost awake and that it was not too late. Patsy's eyes were wide open with alarm as she helped keep Deirdre upright, patting her sharply and intermittently on either cheek as she did so and talking, talking urgently, begging her to wake up.

The ambulance took ten minutes to arrive and Marion, with the two Labradors, followed it to the hospital in her car. The terrier was left in Patsy's kind and capable hands.

Goodness knows what cocktail of pills Deirdre had swallowed or what exactly her frame of mind had been when she did so. She remembers wanting neither to die nor to live. She remembers waking in the early hours and knowing that unaided she would not go back to sleep. She remembers the silence of the house and the emptiness in her heart. She remembers blackness, bleakness and despair. She does not remember thinking about Harvey, nor does she remember wishing to punish him. She remembers thinking the world would be a better place without her and she remembers wanting oblivion. She remembers very clearly not wanting to go home with Marion, which in the event she did not do, because after twenty-four hours spent in a general ward, she was sent to the Valley Hospital to be treated for depression.

Even in her darkest hour she was able to raise a faint smile at the thought of being incarcerated with the man on a green bicycle who had turned up – or so she thought – to mend a mowing machine.

Two weeks later, on the day that Deirdre left the Valley Hospital, she looked up at the stars and said to herself, 'Never again.' Never again would she allow such a thing to happen to her. Never again. That day marked a turning point in her life.

While all this had been going on, Harvey had, of course, been ordering up more and more bull shots and pecan pies, living the life of Riley, blissfully unaware of anything beyond his own immediate physical desire. But Frances, as it later turned out, was beginning to weary of pecan pies and – more than that – she was beginning to worry about what was happening to George.

George had written to her and – much to Harvey's indignation – had telephoned her more than once at the Algonquin. The burden of his song was that he would wait so long but no longer. He did not want to lose Frances – wanted her to come back because he loved her but considered that as a mother she was falling short of the ideal. He felt he could forgive anything but doubted his ability to do so in, say, a year's time.

Harvey didn't want to have to think about George; even less did he wish to think about Frances's children.

Frances said that when they returned home, she would

have to see the children and she would have to see George too, if only to explain that she hadn't meant to fall in love with Harvey, and to apologize. Of course, she swore she would not go back to him. How on earth could Harvey possibly imagine that she ever would?

Harvey has never believed in apologizing for anything. It is difficult to think that he didn't then feel the carpet slipping from under his feet. Neither, for that matter, do I think that Frances is a great one for apologizing, but then between her and George there has always existed something special, something which she must surely have missed with Harvey and which she must have known George to be missing. Perhaps, too, she had broken the bounds of some private agreement between the two of them. Perhaps, she was allowed so much licence, but only so much. Perhaps this time she had gone too far.

Back in London people were taking bets as to which of the two men would finally win Frances. If it was Harvey, then victory – or so most people felt – would be short-lived. No one could imagine Frances putting up with his nonsense for long. It would be a Pyrrhic victory: she would be gone again before he could turn around.

Harvey, of course, had no idea at this time that Deirdre was having a nervous breakdown, had taken an overdose and was languishing in the Valley Hospital.

I suspect that Harvey is so deeply involved with himself and his own affairs that, for him, other people cease to exist when they are out of his sight. I doubt that during all the time he was in New York he ever so much as gave Deirdre a passing thought. Had he, he could not have done so without compunction. Leave your wife, but do not choose to presume that she no longer exists.

On arriving in London he and Frances must have had

some doubt as to where they should go. Even Harvey must have begun to worry about endless hotel bills, which back in England would have seemed more threatening and real than they ever did in the cloud-cuckoo-land that was the Algonquin. Somehow, the two of them had to resume some sort of real life.

For two days they stayed at the Hyde Park Hotel with Harvey really beginning to worry about the cost, longing for Shackles – or at least for the money that Shackles would realize. They told no one that they were back, but then Frances wanted to go shopping and even evinced a faint curiosity about her children, beginning to realize that she couldn't reasonably expect to spend the rest of her life in a hotel bedroom. Harvey Nichols was there to tempt her, on the other side of the street . . . She told Harvey that she needed to go there, to buy shoes – a dress – who knows what?

In Harvey Nichols she met a friend and then the spell was broken. It seemed, according to that friend, that the reality, such as it was, of her rather spoilt existence suddenly bore in on her. Suddenly she wondered what she was doing and what on earth she was about to do. Perhaps she even thought of her children. Certainly she must have thought of George, who had probably never been completely banished from her mind. She no doubt thought of Harvey too and, who knows, realized then and there that a future with him was not a viable proposition. In any case, what she did was to go back to George.

The news spread in a flash. Telephone lines around the country buzzed with speculation about what Harvey would do next. The gossips were in their element.

Harvey, to tell the truth, was left looking an awful fool, alone with his suitcase in the Hyde Park Hotel. In the end he had no alternative, for the time being, but to return to Shackles and face the music, which involved discovering what had happened to Deirdre.

When he did discover, he was most annoyed. There is no other way to describe his reaction. Deirdre, he was convinced, had made an attempt on her life purely to punish him. It was hardly his fault if they locked her up in a bin as a result; her behaviour could only reinforce his conviction that he had been right to leave her. His main preoccupation at the moment was to get Frances back, which he felt certain he would be able to do once he had sold the house and farm and found somewhere else for them to live. In the meantime he would take a furnished flat in London. It annoyed him to think that out of the sale he would have to provide for Deirdre. He didn't feel she had earned it – after all, they had no children and had only been married for a handful of years. It wasn't his fault that she hadn't much money of her own. The most valuable thing she had, in fact, was a diamond and sapphire bracelet given to her by Harvey's mother as a wedding present.

Deirdre was out of hospital, recuperating with her parents in Lincolnshire, apparently well on the way to recovery and thinking positively. Harvey, meanwhile, desperate for Frances, talking about her all the time to anyone and everyone and convinced that he would get her back because, he said, their love was something special, was settled in a bachelor pad in Chelsea. On every side he appeared to be frustrated: by Deirdre, by the failure to sell Shackles and most of all by Frances – or, as he fondly believed, by George, whom he blamed entirely for Frances's defection.

For a while Harvey tried to dismiss any financial worries he might have from his consciousness, but somewhere under the surface there must have been a niggling awareness of the difficulties he was running into or he would surely never have come up with the idea of burgling Shackles.

When friends exclaimed later at his temerity, he replied without a qualm that he could hardly presume that taking an heirloom which he regarded as his by right might be described as burglary.

But, people said, didn't he break into the house while Deirdre was still in Lincolnshire? Didn't he arrange the whole thing so that it looked like an outside job? Weren't the police called, and didn't Harvey lie low for a while, leaving the police to waste their precious time and go on a wild-goose chase after a bunch of local lads?

Harvey denied nothing. In fact he was very proud of his coup, boasted about it endlessly, about how, eventually, he'd persuaded the pretty little policewoman that he'd broken in only because he had lost his keys. What explanation he gave for the fact that all Deirdre's clothes had been tipped out of the drawers and left in untidy heaps all over the floor, I really don't know. I can only presume that eventually the police must have decided that it was a domestic affair and therefore no concern of theirs.

As for Deirdre, she never wished to pursue any discussion as to the rightful ownership of the bracelet. She wasn't interested in diamonds and felt that if Harvey wished to stoop so low, he was welcome to keep the beastly bracelet. She hoped the stolen goods would burn his fingers.

Harvey's mother was very angry indeed when she eventually heard about it. The bracelet did not belong to Harvey. He had no right whatsoever to take it.

Chapter VI

Perhaps it was just as well for Mrs Hotham that she died before she ever came to hear the story of Harvey's exploits with Zed.

At some point in her life the poor woman must have been confronted by the possibility that her younger son was not the prodigy she had long dreamed him to be. For all his promise and for all her hopes pinned so high, he never played cricket for Surrey, his farming had been a disaster, his marriage a catastrophe, a cloud hung over his time in the army, he failed to get the degree he'd predicted for himself, failed to look after his inheritance, was remarkable more for his buoyancy than for anything else. Yet despite all this and much more which must have been painful to Harvey's mother, she persisted until the end in believing that somehow he would prove her right.

Harvey, she would declare with the wilful blindness of the doting mother, was a very sensitive person – or an especially gifted one, a man of great imagination, whose many talents made it hard for him to discover the right path in life.

'The thing about my younger son, Harvey,' she would be

heard to say, 'is that he is an extraordinarily generous person.' Or a very brave one, or exceptionally gifted at languages. God alone knows where she got these ideas from, fishing frantically in a lake of talents, wondering what she would come up with next – surprising herself no doubt as she searched desperately for something that would stick. He was a wonderful son, a man of integrity, with an eye for a ball, a fine palate, an ear for music, attractive to women . . .

If she was occasionally taken off her guard on learning about something particularly preposterous that Harvey had done, and so could not think quickly enough to protect him, then – as with the theft of the bracelet – the disappointment that had lain for years carefully buried under layer after layer of self-deception, would break through and express itself in a sharp burst of bitter anger which would soon give way to silent disapproval.

It was Janey, Harvey's sister-in-law, who first discovered about the sale of the bracelet. Her husband, John – Harvey's older brother – had taken over the Ayrshire property long before old Mr Hotham died, and neither Janey nor he came south very often. John, as is so often the case with the unpreferred child, has always been serious, reliable, thoughtful, hard-working, a man who carefully and dutifully looked after his ageing father and subsequently his widowed mother when she went to live in what was once the gardener's cottage, as well as his estate. Mrs Hotham was already nearly seventy when she was widowed and so decided that it was too late for her to retire to her beloved France. Far better for her to remain where she was, indifferent neighbour to an unloved son and a handful of grandchildren. Janey she never liked very much because Janey, she felt instinctively, spelled trouble. Trouble of the sort which usually involved Harvey.

Janey is small, Scottish and tough. She has always had little if any time for her brother-in-law. Harvey, she thinks, is quite the most selfish person she has ever come across in her life and so she has never been able to understand why it was that her mother-in-law abjectly doted on him. Besides which she has usually felt furiously jealous on behalf of her kind, considerate husband who did so much for his mother and who received only put-down remarks, veiled insults and self-pitying complaints in return.

To John it was all water off a duck's back. From earliest youth he had trained himself to step back emotionally from his mother so that her barbed darts invariably struck wide of the mark. As he grew older he taught himself to be sorry for her – living as she did in her own personally designed version of hell – and so was able effortlessly to assume the mantle of a dutiful son. He used to laugh at Janey overreacting to every one of his mother's taunts and to her every paean of praise for Harvey.

John and Janey were the ideal son and daughter-in-law, forever concerned about Mrs Hotham's welfare, visiting her regularly and ensuring that everything about the house was well looked after for her. Whatever Janey may have felt, or said behind her mother-in-law's back, she did her best to behave well and to conceal her irritation when she saw her, which does not mean that she was incapable of standing up for herself, speaking out when she deemed it necessary and making her own position absolutely clear. Harvey, on the other hand, rarely visited his mother.

He was always promising to come next week – next month – as soon as he could possibly get away. Even when he had made a plan that sounded more or less definite, he generally forgot about it as soon as he had put the telephone down, leaving his mother, overjoyed at last, convinced that her precious boy was on his way, only to be disappointed yet again. Harvey, Mrs Hotham would tell her friends, was a particularly loving son and always had been. John, she often said quite openly, was cold, whereas darling Harvey had a genuinely warm heart. It was a pity of course that Harvey lived in the south because it was difficult for him to come home often. On the rare occasions when Harvey did put in an appearance north of the border, it was usually because either Janey or John had begged him to come – not to say nagged him.

Janey would be forthright and simply tell him that she did quite enough for his mother and that it was high time he stopped leaving everything to her and John and made some sort of an effort himself. John would say, more gently – and more generously perhaps – that Harvey should come for their mother's sake.

'You know how she worships you. Don't let her down. She's old and lonely.'

Harvey used to be infuriated. As far as he could see, John had inherited their father's property and along with it all the responsibility for their mother. Of course he was fond of his mother, but it was hardly his fault that she lived in Scotland. Nobody could reasonably expect him to go running up and down to Scotland every ten minutes. His mother, he said, was a very demanding woman with nothing to do but to think of herself. With John's family next door, she had no excuse for being lonely.

I remember how he used to groan at Shackles when Deirdre told him that his mother wanted him on the telephone. He complained that she talked too much but then, when you heard him pick up the receiver, he would start to talk and carry on talking without drawing breath until he finally said goodbye, telling her about this and that and what delicious food they were eating and inventing a lot of nonsense about how busy he was and how he couldn't wait for a chance to get away and how he longed to see her, and telling her silly jokes which he had up his sleeve and which we had all heard a dozen times in a variety of versions.

After Frances left Harvey, he did in fact go back to Scotland for a few days. Perhaps he had nowhere else to go at a time when he must have been feeling badly let down, may even have realized that he had made a bit of a fool of himself. With his back up against the wall, he knew where to go to be admired, praised, taken seriously, sided with and listened to. He instinctively knew where the best place was for him to retire and lick his wounds.

So for a few days Mrs Hotham was happy listening to her son, readily convinced that Harvey had been quite right to leave Deirdre, whom she felt she had never really got to know but whom she had always thought not good enough for him – neither clever enough nor smart enough nor pretty enough. She sympathized deeply with her son over Frances, believing the whole saga to be nothing more nor less than proof of what she had always known, that Harvey was a very sensitive man, passionate and deep, capable of true love. She listened to Harvey analysing Frances in a way entirely to suit himself and allowed herself to be persuaded that Frances could not possibly have gone back to George for good but that she would certainly return to Harvey before very long. She even suggested that Harvey might like to bring Frances to stay in Ayrshire.

Harvey agreed to do so, but the plan never came to fruition.

Frances's defection was one of the biggest batterings Harvey had ever suffered – may ever have suffered yet – for he had staked so much on her and on their great love as though he had seen himself magnified by it and his existence ratified. He could not believe that she could so calmly and so suddenly turn her back on it all and return as if it were nothing to her silent husband. Apart from anything else Harvey, having been spoilt all his life, was quite unaccustomed to not having his own way and totally incapable of understanding why he shouldn't have it. For some time after returning from Scotland he continued to talk as though Frances was definitely coming back to him, saying that she was only with George temporarily in order to sort things out and to see her children. He referred to Frances (who was after all living with her husband) and himself as 'we' – in the way that married couples say 'we'.

People were generally embarrassed when they heard him say, 'We're looking for a house in World's End' or 'We hope you'll come and see us as soon as we've found somewhere.' Occasionally people who were behind the times with the gossip presumed that he was referring to Deirdre and that he and she were getting together again.

It was during this period that Janey came to London to see an old school friend who had moved south, and for a few days' shopping. Her friend, who had recently inherited some snuffboxes from an aunt, asked Janey to accompany her round to Sotheby's to have them valued and while they were there they happened to look at some jewellery which was due to be sold the next day. To her amazement Janey recognized Deirdre's bracelet. She hadn't seen it very often but she had known of its existence ever since she married John and up to a point had kept a beady eye on it. Then it had been given to Deirdre as a wedding present. Janey would have recognized that wee trinket anywhere.

At first she presumed that it must be Deirdre who was selling it and in a fit of busybodying indignation she telephoned Harvey to tell him and to ask if he knew what on earth was going on. Harvey, not surprisingly, breezily admitted that it was he who had sent the bracelet to Sotheby's and then produced a rigmarole of inconsequential nonsense which proved irrefutably to him that it was his in fact and that he had an absolute right to sell it. When Janey coldly demanded what Deirdre thought about that, he blithely replied that she probably didn't even realize about the sale since he hadn't thought it necessary to tell her. He then cheerfully explained how it was that he had broken into Shackles and taken the bracelet, which he said he had done to avoid a row. Had he asked Deirdre for it, she might quite unreasonably have refused to hand it over.

Janey was perfectly furious, thinking too of how that jewel might have been hers to pass on to her own daughter-in-law. She felt that Harvey ought to be made to withdraw the bracelet from the sale and with this in mind she tried first to contact Deirdre, who was in Lincolnshire with her parents recuperating from her stay in hospital and in no fit state to be worrying about bracelets. In fact, I learned later, Deirdre was so disgusted by the whole episode that she put it from her mind as quickly as she could, refusing to take any action against Harvey, and decided that the outmoded object which she would never dream of wearing was in any case ill-omened and she was better off without it. She no longer wanted to be dependent on the Hothams for her welfare and decided that as soon as she was well enough, she would take control of her life and earn her own living, however hard that might prove to be.

Infuriated at the lack of response from Deirdre, Janey decided that it was incumbent upon her to report the whole episode to her mother-in-law, which she did against her husband's advice. What, John wanted to know, did she hope to achieve by such an action? The bracelet had by this time been sold and Harvey must have pocketed a handsome cheque – short of calling in the police, there was nothing further to be said about the matter.

In Janey's view, Harvey should not be allowed to get away with it. That was all. And, John suspected, his poor mother should not be allowed to get away with believing for ever in her younger son. Janey would not have it. Perhaps in the darker recesses of Janey's mind there may have lingered a sneaking hope that Mrs Hotham would be so disgusted by Harvey's behaviour and by the pocketing of his ill-gotten gains that she would favour her grandchildren in the final distribution of her wealth, refusing further to endow him. Janey is nothing if not fiercely defensive of her children's interests.

Mrs Hotham's first reaction on hearing about the sale of the bracelet was to be very angry with Janey. The whole thing had nothing at all to do with Janey, who was informing, Mrs Hotham rightly suspected, in order to put mother against son and possibly to advance the cause of her own singularly uninteresting brood. She snapped at Janey, refused to say a word against Harvey and changed the subject, turning her attention instead to the misdemeanours of her grandchildren. One had not thanked for a birthday present, another had never read a book, a third seemed lacking in curiosity – never listened when you spoke to it. Children, of course, were no longer properly brought up no matter who their parents might be. One thing to be said for her own children was that they had always had excellent manners – like French children. French children always had such good manners. On and on she went.

But the seed had been sown. When Janey left her after a cup of tea, Mrs Hotham's thoughts must have turned back to what she had heard. No doubt she was very angry, with an anger provoked not so much by what Harvey had done as by being forced herself to confront that delinquency. She ever avoided facing up to the truth about Harvey and any attempt to force it on her generally rendered her temporarily incapable, sending her into a downward spiral of depression.

The result on this particular occasion, as it had been not infrequently in the past, was that Mrs Hotham battened down the hatches, refused to see John or Janey for a while, ignored her grandchildren and, above all, shunned any contact with Harvey. At times like this she hated even to think about him and if anyone did happen to mention him to her, her replies would be brief and bitter. Of course it was easy for her to have nothing to do with Harvey since he so rarely contacted her: she had merely to refrain from telephoning him, which at other times she did on a regular basis.

I'm not sure how long after this it was that Mrs Hotham became ill, or whether she had ever really made friends again with Harvey, but I do remember that Harvey at this time was forever complaining about his mother – about how selfish she was and how difficult. He began to invent a past for her, lovers of whom I feel sure she had never dreamed. Away he would go, stammering as the pace of his speech accelerated, talking of doctors with names like MacRae and MacPherson and ghillies called Douglas and pastors with stern Lowland Scots names. Faithless she had been to his poor old father – suddenly Harvey loved his father inordinately. He was, I suppose, trying to punish her for his own fall from grace because Harvey, I have often noticed, could never bear to be out of favour with his mother although he would never have admitted so much, and although he never lifted a finger for her but complained about her when he thought she was forever around his neck.

I remember hearing that when he was told of her illness,

he brushed the news aside with the remark that she was a very manipulative woman who was no doubt trying only to draw attention to herself. If she was really ill, of course he would go up to Scotland to see her, but he had no reason to suppose that there was anything the matter at all. When she was taken to hospital in Glasgow, he refused to entertain the idea for a single moment that there might be any cause for concern. People of her age were always going in and out of hospital for check-ups. They had nothing else to do but to worry about their health. All her life his mother had had remarkably good health; he was sure that there was nothing the matter with her now and was intensely irritated by Janey's endless fussing.

In fact, before long Janey gave up trying to contact Harvey about his mother. She was so angry with him that she could barely remain civil when she spoke to him and besides, if he didn't come to his mother's sickbed, then Mrs Hotham would finally have to face up to the truth about him. Janey was never quite sure of exactly what effect the story about the bracelet had ultimately had on her mother-in-law – and then again her children's interests were probably never far from the forefront of her mind.

Mrs Hotham came out of hospital and returned home with little prospect of her health improving. She had a bad heart condition with a prognosis that she was unlikely to live for more than a year or two. She was having a certain amount of difficulty in getting around, certainly in climbing the stairs, and suffered increasingly from shortage of breath. Janey was worried about her living alone and foresaw the day when she would have to take her to live with her and John. She did not relish the idea.

Perhaps it was that Harvey was angry with his mother for being ill, that somewhere in the back of his mind he felt her condition served her right for her treatment of him. I happen to think that Harvey was afraid to see his mother in her weakened condition. For – to him at least – she had always represented strength. The idea of seeing her pale and angry and shrunken, confronting death, was not one which he could easily entertain. Neither would he himself have been prepared to confront the idea of her death. He would have preferred to blot out what was happening in Scotland and to carry on with his easy-come-easy-go lifestyle in London. Besides, now that he was beginning to get over Frances, it was easy to imagine how little he would have liked to go back to visit a mother with whom, childlike, he had last taken refuge in a time of distress, and in whom he had confided his love of Frances. He had shown his vulnerability and he wouldn't have wanted to be reminded of it.

More than a year must have gone by before Mrs Hotham eventually died, during which time Harvey never went to see her once. I heard that she eventually became very weak indeed, spending large parts of the day lying in bed in a bedroom which had been arranged for her on the ground floor of her cottage since she was almost as reluctant to move in with John and Janey as they were to have her. Not surprisingly she became quite seriously depressed and some said that she longed to die although, on occasions, an almost superhuman optimism led her to believe that she was only temporarily ill and that come the spring – or come Christmas, or come the warmer weather – she would surely be well again.

By this time Harvey's misdemeanour over Deirdre's bracelet had been, if not forgotten, at least relegated to the back of his mother's mind, and as she lay in bed day after day, no doubt mulling over her life in her mind's eye, she began once again to recreate for him the characteristics of an ideal son. Deirdre was now the devil incarnate who had made him so unhappy and Frances was merely a weak woman who, hardly surprisingly, had fallen for Harvey's irresistible charms. Harvey's only fault, Mrs Hotham seemed to be telling friends at the end, was that he was far too trusting, always seeing the best in everyone, which meant that he had a tendency to fall for the wrong women – women who were only out to take advantage of him. It didn't seem so very long since Harvey's name had been unmentionable in his mother's presence; someone had once even heard her remark tartly that it was disgraceful: Deirdre should have taken him to court. Briefly she had felt sorry for Deirdre.

She did so want Harvey to find someone good enough for him at last and to settle down and have children. Harvey would make such a wonderful father – he was such a family man. Perhaps it was in the hopes of seeing this particular dream fulfilled that Mrs Hotham managed to remain alive at all that year.

Once again she had taken to telephoning Harvey regularly, never failing to tell him how she longed to see him, even trying to pin him down to a date.

Sometimes Harvey would say yes, he absolutely promised that he would come on the following weekend, or the first weekend of the next month, but then, just before he was due to go, he would ring with some rigmarole of an excuse to explain why it was impossible for him to leave London. His mother wondered if he had a new girlfriend and even posited the theory that, having learned from his mistakes, he was probably wanting to be very quiet about her until he was quite certain that this time he had found the right person. Little did she know that in London he had a reputation of making a pass at anyone in a miniskirt – which in those days meant most of the female population under the age of forty.

Harvey by then had become something of a laughing stock

among his acquaintances. He would remark that since he and Deirdre were divorced, he could do what he liked, then, with a shrug of his shoulders, bound off after another lissom twenty-year-old or the glamorous, bored wife of one of his friends, often to be rebuffed; but then he laughed and heedlessly went on his way, allowing no such rejections even slightly to dent his overwhelming belief in his own charm and in his power to attract the opposite sex.

Mrs Hotham's voice must have grown weaker as she lay in bed or sat hour after hour in an armchair, breathless from her heart condition. Harvey could not have failed to know that she was genuinely ill but still, as he rang her to wriggle out of yet another promise to come to Scotland, he would tell her how well she sounded, that her illness was entirely in the mind and that all she needed to do was to go for a walk – she'd be sure to feel fine. Sometimes he suggested that she should come to London, he'd take her to the opera, to exhibitions – there were some wonderful things on.

When she pleaded that she really was not well enough for that, even the journey would be too much for her, he'd just tell her to get on a first-class sleeper, then swear that he'd look after her when she arrived. She, poor woman, would interpret that as Harvey being extraordinarily considerate then retreat into her usual state of despondency. Harvey meanwhile, once he had put the telephone down, would be complaining about his mother, saying that she was spoilt, a malingerer. No wonder she was depressed if she never left Scotland – it wasn't his fault that he never saw her, he'd pressed her to come to London but she wouldn't come and the only reason she refused was in order to be difficult, to try to make him feel guilty. Of course if she was really ill he would go like a flash but, as it was, he didn't really see why he should allow her to manipulate him. And with that he was off – after another miniskirt.

But women were no longer taking him seriously and, in fact, at around that time, Harvey was having an affair with a rather plain girl he'd picked up in an estate agent's office. I think she'd shown him around one or two properties when he was looking for somewhere to live. It was a sort of open secret about this girl, whose name I can't even remember. It might have been Jilly. But funnily enough I can still see her absolutely clearly with her low, broad brow, snub nose and inanely cheerful expression and can hear her cackling laugh. She was a big girl with large thighs and unshapely legs who should have longed for the fashion to change – for the miniskirt to be out – not that she appeared to be remotely self-conscious in any way. Perhaps that was what Harvey liked about her. Perhaps she exemplified the theory that plain girls are usually very keen. Perhaps he liked her too because she made him feel superior by allowing him to treat her in the most unchivalrous fashion, like some kind of hired whore who would be there when he wanted her and disappear as soon as she was in the way.

Some people felt sorry for Jilly, thinking that Harvey treated her badly, but I'd say that to a certain extent she asked for it. Whether or not she entertained the idea of marrying him, I have no idea but I would rather think not. She gave the impression more of being a good-time girl, always laughing too loudly, always ready for another drink, always hoping for another dirty joke, spouting platitudes and bouncing up again when snubbed, like one of those little wooden dolls with lead in their feet. Harvey used to cart her around with him as if she were some kind of cumbersome dog. Then at other times she'd be told, in no uncertain terms, to push off. That was whenever Harvey thought she might be going to embarrass him in front of some of his smarter friends.

Harvey and Jilly were supposed to be going off to Brighton for what Harvey with his old-fashioned attitude to sex chose to call a 'dirty' weekend, when John rang to say that Harvey really must come up to Scotland at once. Mrs Hotham's condition had seriously declined and it was feared that it was now only a matter of days. There was a nurse in attendance and she was very weak, able to speak for only a short time at once.

Even this emergency failed to move Harvey; or at least Harvey refused to allow the reality of it to infiltrate his brain. Apart from anything else, it has to be said that he was quite set on his weekend in Brighton with Jilly. He convinced himself that once again Janey was trying to make him feel guilty, she was only twisting his arm, having worked herself up, and had persuaded John to intervene. How on earth could they suddenly announce that his mother was on her deathbed? She'd been perfectly all right up till now; in fact last time he'd seen her she was fine and that, he swore, was only a couple of months ago – well, it might have been a little longer.

But somewhere, deep inside, his conscience must have stirred because he did eventually agree to go north after the weekend. He even went so far as to book a flight to Glasgow on the Monday afternoon. Just to keep them all quiet, he said. What reason he gave John for not coming sooner, I cannot imagine; no doubt he invented some long incomprehensible account of mysterious business deals and of people who absolutely could not be let down – people who were coming over especially from G-Germany for discussions . . .

In any case, as was inevitable, Mrs Hotham died on the

Saturday night without ever again setting eyes on her darling, sensitive, talented younger son who at that very moment, despite having been summoned to her side, was cavorting in bed in Brighton with a plain, fat girl from Winkworth's whom he was, as it happened, never to see again.

I remember being rung early on the Sunday morning. John and Janey were desperate to contact Harvey and were telephoning all his friends to see if they could trace him. Whatever lie he had told them certainly didn't hold water as they were unable to understand why he wasn't at home. Someone, when they realized the gravity of the situation, told John that they thought Harvey had gone to Brighton for the weekend – to stay in a hotel. Heaven knows what construction John and Janey were to put on that, but, in any case, they apparently began ringing around all the hotels in Brighton until they finally caught up with him.

'I was actually on the job when the call came through,' Harvey told someone. 'God knows how they found out where I was.' Somehow Harvey managed to turn the story round to deflect – or so he persuaded himself – criticism from his own behaviour by highlighting the stranger aspects of the story and by further gross exaggeration or shocking revelation.

Since John had rung me when he was trying to find Harvey, and since Janey had rung again later asking me to the funeral, I thought that I ought to go although it was so far away. But as it was to be on a Friday afternoon and as I had an old bachelor uncle living in Glasgow whom I hadn't seen for years, I decided to take the sleeper up on Thursday night and spend the rest of the weekend with my uncle. Which is what I did.

The church was packed for the funeral. All those ghillies and doctors and pastors, all the MacRaes and MacPhersons from years gone by, singing 'Abide with me', Harvey remarked flippantly at the wake. But his mother, though a difficult woman and, no doubt, a sad one, had lived in Ayrshire all her adult life, had involved herself in local affairs and was well regarded in the neighbourhood. She knew a great many people and had a great many friends in different walks of life.

Even the tough little Janey wept at the graveside and conceded that her mother-in-law had had her good points too. But Harvey was extraordinary. I watched him covertly as he pranced around his old home – now his brother's house – offering wine and sandwiches as if he quite belonged to the place, as if he had never left it and as if the whole world must admire him. He was centre stage. He had lost his adored mother. Somehow John didn't count. Of course, as far as Harvey is concerned, John never has counted.

But there was something deeply uncomfortable for anyone who knew Harvey well, in the sight of this hyped-up man whirling around at his mother's funeral, playing to the gallery, alternately making jokes of borderline bad taste and lavishly expressing his sorrow. How he would miss her! What a wonderful person she had been! A truly marvellous mother!

Of course none of this was anything but natural to Harvey. His philosophy of life has always been brazen. When in trouble, show off. And indeed I believe that he was in trouble. He could hardly take in what had happened. What with the shock, Janey's anger directed at him and, presumably, some sort of feeling that he had let his mother down one final time and that now there was no chance of redemption – with her at least – he must have been feeling pretty miserable. Besides which he had lost the one major prop in his life; the one person who, however little he saw her, however badly he treated her, would always believe in him and would always praise him. Someone who had been doing just that all his life, who had always been in the background, a permanent asset, there but not considered, like good health or a straight nose.

So here was Harvey, mourning his mother, full of the usual braggadocio, but with no wife, no girlfriend, no job, a dwindling fortune and apparently very little idea of what he was about. I asked him what his plans were but he misunderstood me, on purpose I think, and said that he would be staying with John and Janey for a day or two – at which he pulled a face – before going back to London. He'd give me a ring some time.

Chapter VII

The outcome of Harvey's trip to Lincolnshire with Zed was, if anything, even more reprehensible than the outcome of the episode concerning the bracelet. What with the misunderstanding over Zed's head-scratching and one thing and another, and Harvey's overexcitement and greed, they eventually came away, against Zed's real advice, having negotiated to buy the so-called Canaletto drawing in the lavatory as well as the little English landscape.

Perhaps Mrs Drew, having fallen on hard times, was desperate for the cash, or perhaps, having become such a recluse and even more self-doubting than before and thus unworldly, she had found it difficult to refuse the offer. Or it could be that she was just a little excited by such an interlude in what was otherwise a most uneventful existence, since now she rarely went anywhere apart from to the shops or to visit a couple of old friends in the neighbourhood. She had discovered that widows and single women living alone in the country are rarely invited out, frequently forgotten after the first two or three months of their bereavement. Her daughters visited her intermittently and once in a blue moon she would go unwillingly to London for some family affair such as a niece's wedding which was, as it happens, what had taken her there on the occasion that she bumped into Harvey in the Fulham Road.

When her daughters heard what Harvey had been up to, they were all furious. Not one of them trusted him, particularly since the affair of the bracelet; but since Mrs Drew must have sensed that they would not approve of what she had done, she never bothered to mention it and no doubt hoped that it would pass quite unnoticed, which is exactly what did happen for nearly a year.

The daughters came and went, but either they didn't use the downstairs lavatory, or they were remarkably unobservant, or perhaps they all merely saw in their minds' eyes what they had always seen and therefore what they expected to see.

Funnily enough, it was Marion who first noticed the absence of the small oil painting in the sitting room. She said that she happened to be staring at that corner of the wall wondering what was odd about it when it dawned on her that there had once been a picture hanging there. In fact, a small square patch of wallpaper, much darker than the rest, showed exactly where it had been.

Marion is probably the least artistically inclined of the three sisters and the one least concerned with interiors. All her interests lie out of doors, with horses, dogs, gardens, tennis and golf. The inside of her house, as I was to discover later, is equipped with all the most up-to-date, labour-saving devices because Marion is incredibly efficient, likes to do things properly but wants them done quickly so that she can get back outside. There is very little that is merely decorative, or if there is, it seems to be there by mistake, either inherited or bought to cover a space on the wall, like the mediocre oil paintings of horses done by an old school friend of Marion's.

She had probably never bothered to look closely at the landscape painting in her parents' sitting room, even less at the pen-and-ink drawing in the lavatory.

Deirdre was amazed when she heard that they had both gone, particularly since she had been twice to her mother's house without having noticed their absence. I think she was rather annoyed that it should have been Marion who was the first to notice. Deirdre had always been particularly fond of that little painting and had often urged her mother to have it cleaned. How could she not have missed it?

Anyway, as Marion stared at the patch on the wall where it had been, she couldn't even remember what used to be there. All she could remember was something small and dark. If you had asked her whether it was a picture of a building, an interior or the sea, she would have had no idea.

'What used to hang there?' she asked her mother, pointing sharply at the empty space.

Mrs Drew was refilling her sherry glass at the time and didn't instantly take in what Marion was asking, but when her daughter repeated the question, she looked a bit shifty, said something vague and tried to change the subject. Eventually she admitted that she had sold the picture that used to be there and then made quite a thing out of her surprise that Marion couldn't remember it. How unobservant Marion must be! No doubt she was trying to avoid any too close questioning as she would not have wanted to bring Harvey's name into the discussion.

Marion saw no reason why her mother shouldn't sell her own picture if she felt like it, especially as she knew quite well that her father had left his widow in straitened circumstances, but she did feel that Mrs Drew's manner indicated that there was more to the story than she was prepared to reveal. Besides, it struck her as odd that her mother had never bothered to mention the fact of the sale. She spoke to her daughters fairly often and generally had very little to report, having been nowhere and seen no one. The sale of a picture must have been an event in her life.

When Marion got home she telephoned both her sisters to see if either of them knew anything about it all. It was then that Deirdre realized that the 'Canaletto' had gone as well. It was so strange, she had obviously noticed its absence without registering it, but now she felt sure that it too had gone. Had Marion looked in the downstairs lavatory?

Naturally Marion couldn't remember what the drawing looked like either, despite the fact that Deirdre was able to give her a very accurate description of it; she certainly had no idea whether or not it was still in its usual place.

Deirdre thought for a while after talking to Marion, but did not in the least bit like the way her thoughts were taking her. She knew perfectly well that Harvey was now an art dealer and that he was one person who was aware of a *soi-disant* Canaletto, but it seemed inconceivable that her mother would ever have allowed him, of all people, inside her house. Least of all would she have had any serious dealings with him. She tried to put the idea out of her mind.

Meanwhile Marion was busy ringing the second sister, June.

June is the most grasping and money-minded of the three sisters. The kind of person who sees her parents' property while they are still alive as being already hers. She most certainly would not have accepted it as her mother's right to sell anything at all without first consulting her daughters. It was she who had been most vociferous in her anger on hearing about Harvey and the bracelet, urging Deirdre to take him to court. Besides being more grasping and money-minded than her sisters, June was also the one who got on least well with her mother and who, more than the others, tried to tell her mother what to do. In fact June makes a point of trying to tell everyone what to do.

As soon as June had finished talking to Marion, and without further hesitation, despite the fact that she had no clearer picture in her mind than Marion had of either the missing drawing or the painting, she decided to ring her mother.

Mrs Drew was, not surprisingly, somewhat put out by hearing June bossing her down the telephone, asking questions in an aggressive fashion and generally treating her like a criminal, or at least a recalcitrant child. She knew perfectly well that June had never shown any interest in either picture and she very much doubted that she had the faintest idea what she was talking about. June of course wanted to know everything about the sale. When had the pictures been sold? Who had sold them? How much money had they made? She then delivered a lecture on the folly of conducting her affairs in the way that her mother did, and asked her why on earth she had not come to her children for advice.

Mrs Drew managed throughout this conversation to withhold Harvey's name and it was not until some days later when she happened to be talking to Deirdre that she revealed the whole truth. A truth at which Deirdre had already half guessed and concerning which she was wondering whether to take any action. It had not escaped her notice that Harvey had been doing very well for himself lately. Not that she ever saw him, but there are always those who love to pass tidbits of information around in the quarters where they are least welcome.

So although Deirdre had no desire to talk about Harvey or to know what he was up to, she had noticed that people never failed to tell her about him. Why should she now wish to know whether Harvey was rich or poor, successful or not, married or unmarried, promiscuous or celibate? Harvey for her was of the past and belonged in the past; they had no children to bind them inextricably together and very little that they could have shared beyond unhappy memories. Deirdre regarded Harvey as a youthful mistake from which she had learned but on which she preferred to turn her back.

Harvey and Zed between them had in fact made a nice little killing. It is difficult to imagine how they acquitted themselves with even a modicum of dignity at the end of their visit to Mrs Drew, since with their confusion over Zed's signals and the sudden appearance of the 'Constable', it must have been hard for them to know exactly how to proceed.

When Zed was in that downstairs lavatory, he had squinted with great care at the drawing which hung there of a view across the Thames. He'd spent quite some time examining it as minutely as he could under the circumstances, and had finally decided that it was unlikely to be a Canaletto for various reasons, but most particularly because, from what he could deduce through the glass, the paper was not contemporary with Canaletto. So, having flushed the lavatory so as to allay any suspicions Mrs Drew might be entertaining, he intended to return to the drawing room and give the thumbs-down sign, if only he could remember what it was. The drawing was a pretty enough thing, but somewhat lifeless, and he was convinced that it would hardly be worth their while to buy it.

When he got back to the sitting room where Harvey was carrying on in the most unexpected fashion about Egyptian water closets and while he was twisting around, trying not to scratch his head and then scratching it, with his beady eye he suddenly noticed the little landscape painting in the corner and some second sense told him that it was not just good, but very good. He had to look at it more closely.

Harvey by this time was all over the place with excitement about Zed's unwitting endorsement of the Canaletto and meanwhile Mrs Drew was talking about Constable and making her fortune.

In the end Zed and Harvey drove off in their hired car with both pictures wrapped in newspaper in the boot, waving and smiling frantically at Mrs Drew as they accelerated away down the weedy drive.

'Very nice lady,' Zed remarked, grinning even more widely than usual.

Harvey at this stage was convinced that they had a Canaletto in the boot, but he was less delighted by Zed's insistence on taking the landscape painting, since he had categorically declared to Mrs Drew that it was most unlikely to be a Constable on account of the way the clouds were painted.

But Zed explained that it had all been a mistake; the drawing he did not think was a Canaletto, and in any case it was a dull thing, but the little oil painting he was very exciting and Zed was ravished by it. The price they had agreed to pay was nothing – peanuts. Zed kept saying 'peanuts' and laughing all the way to London.

No point, Zed explained quite frankly, in agreeing with the lady that the painting might have been a Constable; they would only have had to pay more for it. Mrs Drew was perfectly happy with what they had given her. 'Very nice lady.'

In fact the pair of them had, as they say, hit pay dirt. It eventually turned out that, having lain in wait for nearly a year, they were able to make an enormous profit by the private sale of a Constable and a Canaletto drawing, both of which went abroad. Deirdre was never able to discover who had bought either picture, nor did she know how authentic the attributions were. It naturally rankled with her that her mother had been so used by Harvey, but since there was nothing she could possibly do by the time she came to discover it, she decided to turn her back on the whole affair. To a certain extent what had happened was entirely Mrs Drew's own fault; in Deirdre's opinion she ought never to have entertained Harvey in the first place.

June was far less easily appeased than Deirdre so it was a long time before she was prepared to let the subject drop, going on relentlessly to her mother about her irresponsibility over the matter and nagging Deirdre for not having had any control over Harvey. All that money which should have been theirs by right had ended up in the pockets of Harvey of all people – and of a ludicrous man with a ridiculous name like Zed.

Harvey would have had no qualms whatsoever about the way he had behaved, would have defended his sharp practice to the hilt, having himself no idea at all why anyone should even bother to question the ethics of such a transaction.

Later I heard that Zed and Harvey fell out disastrously and that Harvey was going around London referring to Zed as a crooked Pole. It must have been at around this time that Harvey was obliged to sell the gallery, everything having suddenly gone rather sour on him in the art world. But of course he should have hung on a bit longer since, thanks to some smart advice from Zed who was no fool, he had made quite a collection of Cornish pictures from the Newlyn School whose prices were destined to soar only a few years later.

But, as was his wont, Harvey wasted no time on regrets. For him the crooked Pole exemplified the art world and he no longer wanted any part in it; he would turn his talents in some other direction. No one ever really knew quite how badly Harvey burned his fingers at that time, but he was full of exaggerated stories of chicanery and double dealing by others, with which he entertained his friends whilst presenting himself as pure white as the driven snow.

At about the same time he had occasion to bump into Deirdre at a drinks party in London. They had not seen each other or had any communication for several years and it is easy to believe that both were somewhat arrested on seeing the other. They must rarely have given each other a thought during the intervening years. Deirdre swears that Harvey did not at first even recognize her and I can quite well believe it.

She, on the other hand, noticed Harvey as soon as he came into the room, partly, no doubt, because of his height but partly too on account of an indefinable aura or presence which Harvey carries everywhere with him. He is the sort of man who, perhaps because of an exaggerated awareness of self and of his own mood – whatever that may happen to be – can somehow make himself felt in an otherwise empty house through closed doors. Harvey always has a need to communicate his mood to those around him, bending them to his whim of the moment, so that when Harvey is happy, then everyone must be happy with him; when he is indignant or angry, everyone else must feel the same; and on the rare days when he is depressed, he expects everyone to follow him into the pit.

On this occasion Harvey arrived at a smallish drinks party in World's End in typical Harvey fashion, blustering with talk, jabbering, stammering, waving his arms about, head and shoulders above those he was with, laughing, twisting, turning, telling of some incident that had just happened to him in the street outside, repeating his own repartee. Deirdre could hardly have failed to be aware of his entrace. She felt a sudden lurch of nausea in the pit of her stomach. The last person she had been thinking about was Harvey and he was the last person she wished to see, indeed she was amazed to see him in those particular surroundings for since their separation they moved in very different circles.

Her first instinct was just to hope that she could fade quietly away into the wallpaper and pass unnoticed by Harvey until the moment when she could decently make a getaway. Then, new woman that she was, she put her shoulders back and thought to hell with that! It was peculiar the way the very sight of Harvey automatically caused her to feel as craven and insecure as she had done in the days of her marriage to him, making it seem that nothing had happened in the years between. As if she had not shaken the dust of Shackles off her feet once and for all. It was like going back as a grown woman to your childhood home and feeling uncomfortably as if you were six years old all over again, talking with ludicrous deference to your parents. Deirdre especially is haunted by this fear of being unable to stand aloof from what has gone before. Yet Deirdre, as it turns out, is a very strong person.

So as soon as she had recovered from the initial shock of seeing Harvey and before he could possibly have had time to notice her, Deirdre decided that the best – indeed the only – thing to do was to walk straight up to him and to say hello, which is precisely what she did.

Harvey, still jabbering away, turned, sensing someone at his elbow, and glanced dismissively at Deirdre as he might have glanced at a secretary bringing him a cup of coffee while he was engaged in discussing some important deal on the telephone.

Not to be disconcerted and with what might almost have

been a flirtatious tilt of the head, Deirdre said, 'I think you were once married to me.'

At this point Harvey did a double take and then immediately changed gear. He threw his arms round her, kissed her, began calling her his darling Deirdre – which was almost more than she could take – and introduced her to the people he was talking to as if she were the Queen of Sheba and as if it were extraordinarily clever of him to have been married to her.

Deirdre laughed – a little coldly, I imagine – then asked him how he was. She said she'd heard a great deal about him lately; that he'd been very successful with his picture gallery. In fact she knew – or at any rate she'd been told – that the gallery had gone up in a puff of smoke and that Harvey had fallen on hard times, had got into trouble for sailing dangerously close to the wind.

'It turned out that I had a good eye,' he said, 'but I made the mistake of getting involved with this little Polish crook – in the end I thought that the best thing would be to sell up. In fact, to be quite frank with you, I'd had enough of that world. So much dishonesty in it . . . I'm thinking of opening a restaurant now – something a little different, you know—'

Deirdre interrupted him to say how sorry she was to hear about the gallery, especially since she knew he'd made several excellent coups – had even made a fortune with an undiscovered Constable, she'd been told.

Harvey laughed – a little uneasily perhaps.

But Deirdre was not going to let it go just like that. She turned to the circle of friends gathered round Harvey and trembling, she claims, as she did so, but with a steady voice, said, 'Did Harvey ever tell you about how, long after we were divorced, he went to see my mother in Lincolnshire and bought two pictures from her for nothing, which he was then able to sell, authenticated, as a Constable and a Canaletto? A very good eye indeed.' She gave Harvey a withering glance and added coolly, 'I could never understand how you managed to persuade Mummy to invite you in.'

There was an awkward hush as Harvey's friends looked desperately around for someone else they knew – anyone to talk to. One by one they moved away, sidled off with no apparent destination, frantic to escape.

But Harvey was soon able to fill the silence they had left; after what was no more than a mere hiccough of discomfiture, he was back in the saddle.

'Your mother was delightful,' he said. 'So warm and welcoming. I was really pleased to see her again. I just happened to be staying up there at the time, you know—'

'With your crooked Polish friend? I didn't realize he lived in Lincolnshire.'

'No – n-no – with some old friends – I don't think you ever knew them, but they breed rare species of owls . . .' Then he was away again, stammering on about bay owls and about typical owls and grass owls and their noiseless flight and did Deirdre know that they used their ears sometimes instead of their eyes for hunting prey? Then he started talking about 'auditory cues' and about how he had heard of an owl in Siberia which had mistaken the sound of a b-b-baby crying for that of a ferret calling its mate.

Harvey's ability to pick up and store the most diverse and esoteric pieces of information about almost any subject has often led to confusion, even among his closest friends who find themselves quite unable to identify the moment of his crossing that sometimes shadow line between fact and fiction.

Deirdre no longer cared. All that was now behind her and as she listened to Harvey blathering on about owls and Siberian ferrets, she suddenly felt strengthened and glad that she had bumped into him again at last. It was as if this meeting would help finally to lay the ghost of her failed marriage. By the time he reached the point of absolutely swearing on his word of honour that everything he was saying was really true, Deirdre had turned on her heel and walked away, leaving him momentarily friendless in the middle of the room as he began to imitate the courtship display of the long-eared owl which claps its wings together as it jumps in the air. Harvey accompanied this performance with a wild to-wit-to-woo which echoed like the cry of an abandoned child among the assembled guests.

Not very long after that, Deirdre was infuriated to have it reported back to her that Harvey had been going around telling everyone that he had recently seen her at a party and how attractive she was looking. It showed what good taste he had always had – he'd almost felt like asking her out. He was sure she would have been delighted; after all, it was she who sought him out at the party, not the other way round. In fact, he admitted that he wasn't sure he would even have recognized her, seeing her there so unexpectedly. She'd changed the way she did her hair – grown older.

'The rat!' was all Deirdre could think of saying.

Part II

Chapter VIII

For years I never saw Harvey, no longer even heard very much about what he was up to. I was living abroad then and so inevitably lost touch with a number of old friends, although of course when I did come home for short spells there would always be someone to put me in the picture and tell me what had been happening to everyone. I'd heard, for instance, that Harvey had gone off to live in the country – Devon or Somerset. But, generally speaking, other concerns were mine and everything to do with Harvey was somehow relegated to the past – perhaps even to those days of heedless youth which Harvey has always managed to personify.

It was towards the end of the eighties that I finally came back for good to settle in London, at first feeling quite rootless and at a loss as to where and how to pick up the strands of my life. The years abroad had left me out of touch and out of time. I, too, by now, had a broken marriage behind me, which was one of the things which precipitated my return to this country, leaving my spouse behind in younger, newer arms. Initially I had looked forward to my homecoming, imagining it would soothe the pain of my unhappiness, be like a return under some sheltering maternal roof.

But, as I say, friends had scattered and others I had lost touch with. More than that, London had changed. For one thing it had moved perceptibly further west; it had become busier, with shops open at all hours. For another, it had grown noisier, dirtier, greedier, uglier and ruder; yet, inexplicably, foreigners were attracted to it in greater and greater numbers as if it were the centre of all things desirable.

My own house in Notting Hill, which had been let for so many years, had grown shabby; there was rising damp in the kitchen and the front door was warped so that you had to charge at it with your shoulder if you wanted to get in. I was amazed that the tenants hadn't complained more vociferously. To make matters worse, I returned at the end of October, on the weekend that they put the clocks back, ready for the long, lightless winter months ahead.

I had been back for six or seven weeks, Christmas was drawing near and I was drinking a solitary bowl of packet soup accompanied by a whisky and water one evening, when the telephone rang, jolting me out of my melancholy, not to say my self-pitying thoughts concerning the drabness of my house and the pointlessness of doing anything about it when there was no one to do it for or with. I remember cursing as I rose to answer the telephone for such was my frame of mind in those days, that there was no one I could imagine who would be able to raise my spirits.

Certainly I was pleasantly surprised to hear Deirdre's voice at the other end of the line. We hadn't seen each other or spoken for years, had probably last exchanged Christmas cards more than five years earlier. I did, of course, know that she was now a highly regarded consultant paediatrician at one of the big London hospitals.

The way Deirdre changed course after the end of her disastrous but fortunately short-lived marriage to Harvey has always seemed miraculous to me. When I think of the pale, timid bride of all those years ago and then the isolated, childless young wife at Shackles, it seems almost impossible that they are one and the same person as the confident, professional woman of later years.

Deirdre has an explanation for it all, of course; an explanation which indeed seems to be the only possible one. In the days before most girls were generally encouraged to go to university or to follow professions, many a lively intelligence was stifled, leading women by their hundreds of thousands down the pathways of self-doubt and dissatisfaction to depression, as often as not, incapable of knowing what it was that they missed.

According to Deirdre, she remembers weekends at Shackles, everyone laughing while she sat silent by that pretty fireplace in the sitting room, with the dog she used to have in those days on her lap, thinking, Is this it then? Swamped with misery at the prospect of the years ahead. She now says she was lucky not to have had children with Harvey for if she had, she feels she would never have found the time, the energy or possibly even the desire to turn to medicine. It was a particularly long haul for Deirdre who, having left school with nothing more than School Certificate at the age of fifteen, had to start with A levels in her late twenties.

Coming out of her nervous breakdown, sitting in her parents' house in Lincolnshire, she had had time to think things through thoroughly and she knew then – as she had known subconsciously since childhood – that what she really wanted was to be a doctor. At Shackles, in her loneliness, she had flirted with the idea of taking up painting, inspired perhaps by that trip to Italy. But she knew, even at the time, that it was only a fleeting enthusiasm, one which she was not sufficiently talented to pursue and which at the time served as some kind of analgesic. In those days the possibility of studying medicine would have seemed remote indeed.

But Deirdre well remembers how, even as a very small girl, she used to be fascinated by a sheep's skeleton found in the fields or by the corpse of a rotting rat on the roadside. Her mother used to complain that she showed a morbid interest in such things and was once, she remembers, quite unreasonably cross on finding Deirdre standing in the potting shed, transfixed as she watched the gardener gut and skin a rabbit.

Later, of course, Mrs Drew recognized that what she had formerly seen as an unhealthy obsession was no more than an incipient interest in biology, so that she was eventually able to become immensely proud of her third daughter. To the amazement of almost everyone who knew her, Deirdre managed, after recovering from her breakdown, to cast off the constraints and conventions of her upbringing, to withstand the hard years of training and the exhaustion of the long hospital hours and so establish herself as a professional woman.

June, of course, strongly supported by Marion, was foremost in discouraging any idea of Deirdre's becoming a doctor; both sisters, no doubt, liking to see their younger sibling as weak and in need of their protection – not to say their advice at all times. Furthermore they must certainly have been afraid of her breaking away from what they saw as the norm, soaring to worlds unknown, to realms beyond their understanding. They were convinced that Deirdre was frail; she couldn't begin to cope with the work and even to attempt it might cause another breakdown. Had they ever been prepared to listen, they would have been totally incapable of beginning to comprehend Deirdre when she explained that what had led to that initial collapse was her own unquestioning acceptance of the very norm which they continued to advocate. She had been bitterly unhappy, wanting at an early age to be a boy merely because she had already observed that in life boys had so many more opportunities.

At school Deirdre had been quite good at science but no one had appeared to notice, let alone to encourage her, so meekly she had followed the path cut out for her by her parents and blindly trodden by her sisters before her. She had learned to type and had married – and look where that had led!

Nowadays I think Deirdre would say that Harvey leaving her merely precipitated a nervous breakdown which was the catalyst for a later, extremely successful career. And in the end, of course, June and Marion were always the first to come begging for professional advice, eager to bypass their own GPs and other medical advisers.

In any case Deirdre's voice on the telephone that evening as I sat alone in Notting Hill, feeling an emptiness all around me, came as a pleasant surprise. She had heard, she said, that I was back in London and on my own and had indeed been meaning to get in touch for several weeks. She hadn't forgotten that I had gone to be with her all those years ago when Harvey left and she was so unhappy. But as time went by she kept putting off ringing me, thinking she'd do it the next day, then thinking she'd do it after Christmas until, suddenly, that very evening she'd thought that if she didn't ring soon, she might never get round to doing it at all. She'd had no idea of my address or telephone number – didn't know that I'd kept the house in Notting Hill, but just in case, had rung the number she'd found in an old address book.

'It must be difficult coming back after all these years,' she said and I was touched by what seemed a rare understanding. Most people appeared to think that what with a house to move back into, there could hardly be any problem.

We arranged to meet and when we did, I was struck by how well she looked – prettily dressed, her hair expensively streaked. Fine bones have always lent grace to Deirdre's figure and elegance to her profile, but now she had an added confidence and her soft brown eyes had lost their old world-weariness. From that meeting my life gradually took off again. Deirdre put me in touch with old friends I hadn't seen for years, and introduced me to new ones, even invited me to join a family Christmas in her Berkshire cottage on the edge of the Downs.

The cottage is long and low, built of brick and flint with a thatched roof; the sort of house you see on a jigsaw with hollyhocks growing up beside the front door and an apple tree in the garden. There should really be a white goose under the apple tree and a child in a bonnet with a hoop by the gate. The inside of the cottage was then – is now still – a jumble of books and papers and higgledy-piggledy, undistinguished furniture; there are some pretty old prints of birds and dissected beetles on the walls as well as one or two attractive watercolours of country churches or fields and trees, and a bold, rather surprising abstract hanging a little crookedly over the sitting-room fireplace. All so unlike the orderly, lavish chintz of Shackles. Deirdre laughed as she remembered Shackles. She wouldn't have time for all that fussy nonsense now. All she wanted was somewhere not too far from London where she could go to escape from the pressures of work and be with her family; somewhere in open countryside so that she could go for long walks.

Deirdre's immediate family consisted of her second husband, to whom she had by this time been married for nearly twenty years, but whom I had never met, and a fifteen-year-old son, Will, whose birth had momentarily interrupted the smooth upward curve of his mother's career.

Ralph was considerably older than Deirdre, who by then must have turned fifty. He was a quiet, gentle man with old-fashioned good manners who had recently retired from a lifetime spent as a numismatist in the dingy back rooms of important museums, but who still contributed erudite articles on Roman coins of the second century BC to little-known learned magazines. 'Coins,' Deirdre said, 'are his passion. He much prefers them to people.'

However that may have been, I was warmly welcomed by Ralph as an old friend of Deirdre's, and I soon found him easy to talk to and quietly humorous.

Christmas passed agreeably with various people coming and going for drinks and the odd meal and, inevitably, the conversation turned to Harvey. It was Boxing Day morning; Ralph was talking to someone on the telephone and Will was still in bed while Deirdre and I were having breakfast in the kitchen. Outside there was a leaden grey sky with an almost yellow tinge to it; what little light there was barely penetrated the small latticed windows and an icy wind blew off the Downs and wailed around the cottage, whistling through every available chink, under doors and through apparently closed windows. It felt like snow. I couldn't help remembering Harvey in his farming days, throwing snowballs at a Guernsey bull and shouting 'Olé' from a doubtful position of safety behind a tree.

Harvey to Deirdre now seemed so long ago that he had almost acquired the quality of a mythological creature around whose quasi-magical persona endless cautionary tales are woven. Stories which years ago would have wounded Deirdre to the quick, now had the power to make her laugh – albeit with a bitter-sweet laugh, for Deirdre has a kind heart and then still had a lingering compassion for Harvey whom she had so clearly outstripped – Harvey forever striving to be what he was not, striving to prove himself to others as a means of proving himself to himself, wriggling out of trouble, seeking his own advantage, making a fool of himself over and over again.

Only recently Deirdre had heard an astonishing account of Harvey's nearly being court-martialled during his military service in Cyprus over an incident concerning a brother officer's pistol which he was supposed to have borrowed and left on a chair in a restaurant in Larnaca. Somehow – the true facts are lost in the mists of time – Harvey managed to lie his way out of a tight corner and the charges against him were miraculously dropped. Deirdre was amazed that she had never heard the story before and was curious to know whether or not there was any truth in it.

'Someone ought to write a book about Harvey's misdemeanours,' she said with a laugh.

I did vaguely remember hearing something about a pistol and Harvey and a court-martial, but it was all so many years ago that I could no longer begin to recall the details. I remarked that if I did happen to see Harvey again, there would hardly be any point in asking him about it.

'He'd just lie,' Deirdre said. 'Probably invent some fantastical story to his own glory.'

I reminded her then that there were stories to Harvey's credit – few and far between perhaps. For instance, what about the time another brother officer was shot dead beside him in the street and Harvey walked straight up to the sniper to demand his gun. The Greek – luckily – had run away.

'Foolhardy bravado,' Deirdre said. But then she had to

admit that yes, physically Harvey was not a coward. She wondered if I had made any plans to see him. I said I hadn't but that I would like to get in touch with him at some stage, if only for old times' sake.

'He's got several children,' she said. 'One of them's at school with Will. They're in the same class – play cricket together. Funny, isn't it? As a matter of fact, they're fairly good friends; I'd be quite curious to see him.'

Harvey, it turned out, had not surprisingly been in and out of all sorts of ventures during the intervening years. He'd married again – twice – had even got a child with his new wife, it could hardly be more than two or three years old. Frances, on the other hand, was apparently still with George. Did I remember Frances? And all the fuss there was about her and Harvey?

How could I not remember Frances? Her pretty, pretty face, huge green eyes beneath a sixties fringe; shining, swinging hair. It was hard to imagine her now, though – in her late fifties. She might even be sixty.

Deirdre hadn't seen her for years but she'd heard that Frances had become a pillar of respectability, raising money for the homeless, sitting on committees for abused children and battered wives. One never would have guessed.

'It was another life then,' Deirdre remarked. 'Another world really. I was certainly another person.' After a pause she added, 'So were you,' and gave me a steely look.

Deirdre, I thought at that moment, was a remarkably good-looking woman who bore her years well and with the minimum fuss. I hoped she was happy with Ralph.

I mumbled something about none of us being as young as we once were – times having changed – *et nos . . . in illis . . .*

Then Ralph came back into the room and began to talk

about something his sister had been saying on the telephone and Harvey was immediately forgotten again – relegated to the past, to the story books.

The following day Deirdre had to be at the hospital and I returned to London with her early in the morning. The Downs, as we drove away, were covered with a depressing blanket of ice-white snow; the cottage, its thatched roof sprinkled with a sugary coating of the same, looked the picture of cosy comfort as the cold wind still whistling sent powdery clouds into drifts across the lanes. The prospect of the two months which were to follow filled me with dread and I suddenly longed for the heat and the dirt and the smells of Asia with an almost physical longing.

Back in London I was relieved to find no snow, but the streets were drab and colourless and soon it seemed to me that each succeeding day was barely able to open one sleepy eye before shutting it again in despair as night closed in. People hurried to and from work, shoulders hunched against a cold wind, grim, long-suffering expressions on their faces. It was many years since I had suffered the dreariness of an English winter, so unremitting in its lightlessness, so slow in its progression, in its unalleviated sameness. Looking back to the snowy Downs, I almost longed for a blizzard. Anything to break the monotony.

I counted the days until the clocks would be put forward again and sometimes wondered if I should reach that hallowed date without sinking into terminal depression. As January turned into February, a few early crocuses put in a brave appearance in the park and for a brief moment I deceived myself into thinking that Persephone was at last on her way back from the Underworld. But winter dragged on.

In order to preserve my sanity, I began to devise little treats for myself, to be spaced, like stepping stones, at strategic intervals throughout the weeks that lay ahead, giving me something to look forward to. It occurred to me then that one such treat might involve a reunion with Harvey. When Harvey was not infuriating, at least he usually managed to be entertaining.

A few discreet enquiries soon resulted in my having Harvey's address and telephone number. He was living not far from me in W11. At first I thought of writing to him but then, suspecting that the effort of putting pen to paper might prevent him from answering, I finally decided to telephone; yet such was my apathy that it was some time before I was able to pick up the telephone and actually dial the number. When I did so, the number rang for a while and I was just about – almost with a sense of relief – to ring off, when I heard a click and Harvey's familiar voice said, 'Hello.'

Harvey sounded genuinely pleased to hear me and immediately wished to make a plan to meet. His wife, Moira, was away. She'd gone skiing with a party of friends; Harvey surprisingly hated skiing – never went with her. We agreed to lunch together a couple of days hence.

I was rather glad to see Harvey initially on his own without Moira, so as to be able more easily to catch up with him. All the same I felt a niggling dread as I made my way towards the restaurant where we had arranged to meet. Seeing Harvey now would somehow inevitably dredge up the past, take me back across the years, remind me of long-forgotten incidents which in turn would give rise to long-forgotten feelings, feelings which might be better buried for good. I would no doubt tell him about myself, which would naturally reopen the wounds of the recent past and reawaken an awareness of so many old mistakes and failures.

As I gazed at the pinched faces of the people opposite me on the Underground, I wondered whether I had been wise to contact Harvey and I pondered the nature of friendship. After all, Deirdre was my friend now. Perhaps always had been. Hadn't I grown out of Harvey? Wasn't he just a part of my youth? I could hardly believe that I had anything left in common with him and even asked myself if I had ever really liked him. My tastes had changed in so many ways over the years – if I no longer had the same taste in books and music, why should I have the same taste in friends?

Yet Harvey has an indefinable something, which meant that no sooner had he walked through the door of that restaurant (I was there first, naturally) than I immediately forgot my reservations and was delighted to see him. It was as if we had met yesterday. He looked just the same to me as he had always done, not an extra ounce of flesh, not a grey hair; he was his usual cheerful self with his usual buoyant step.

He had a lot to tell me over that lunch. So much, in fact, that apart from a casual reference to my broken marriage, I hardly spoke about myself at all. Perhaps I had forgotten quite how talkative Harvey is and quite how little he is interested in other people.

Harvey told me so much that day, that lunch stretched well into the afternoon. He spoke mostly of his present involvement in breeding parrots. I was amazed. What on earth would he think of next? But Harvey told me that he was really on to a good thing. Because of the world's busybodies, it was becoming increasingly difficult to import parrots – parakeets, cockatoos, macaws, any of these birds – and yet they were becoming ever more popular as pets. Harvey had a friend down in the country, in Devon or Somerset, somewhere, who had macaws swooping among the beech trees in his garden, yellow and vivid blue, scarlet and green with huge wingspans and white rubbery faces. They settled on the eaves of Harvey's friend's house and pulled the tiles off the roof, caused an enormous amount of damage, terrified the lambs in the fields and bit the neighbour's cat.

I wondered if all that was what people really wanted of a pet. Harvey dismissed my doubts with a wave of the hand and refilled our glasses.

'But just imagine them,' he said, 'putting so much colour into this grey country. That's what everybody wants, isn't it?'

I couldn't imagine these huge birds swooping and screeching in the monochrome of an English winter garden and wondered how they could tolerate the climate. But Harvey assured me that they were perfectly blissful and that he was planning to go into partnership with his friend in Somerset who not only had the know-how but also the space for the venture.

The maximum life expectancy of the hyacinth macaw with its deep-blue plumage and yellow eye-ring is something like sixty-five years, Harvey told me – twice as long as that of a grizzly bear or a pigeon. It occurred to me to wonder whether people really wanted their pets to live quite so long, but not only was he unable to be dissuaded from his plan, but he was quite unperturbed by the possible difficulties involved in encouraging exotic birds to breed in captivity. Harvey had a wonderful vision of macaws and cockatoos eventually nesting in all the London parks and returning at intervals to their owners, who would feed them on fruit and nuts and teach them to sing.

It was not until some time later that I learned how the friend in Somerset, beleaguered by the problems his beautiful birds caused, had been forced to give them to a zoo. He was certainly wise enough, too, not to enter into business with Harvey.

Apart from talking about parrots on that occasion, Harvey

also told me briefly about his life since I had last seen him. He had several children; he'd been married twice – the divorce from his second wife had been a disaster since she had taken not only the very nice house he'd owned at the time, down in the West Country, but most of his money too. He was, he claimed, really on his uppers. If Moira hadn't had a bit of money of her own, God only knew he'd have been in Queer Street. Moira had been married before, too – to a rich bastard. That's where she got her money: took the fellow to the cleaners when she left – quite rightly, in Harvey's opinion. I couldn't quite follow his logic but I said nothing. He was keen for me to meet Moira, of whom he spoke as if she were a new picture he'd acquired, or perhaps a racehorse. She'd be back next week and he wanted me to come over for supper.

I felt obliged to mention Deirdre and to tell Harvey that I'd been seeing her. It was no concern of his, but I would have felt a bit sly if I hadn't said anything about it. I was surprised by his reaction but perhaps I shouldn't really have been. Deirdre, he said, was wonderful. He was proud to have known her. He hadn't seen her for years but it was almost as if he took the credit for her success as a doctor, or as if he felt that it was he who had sat all those medical exams.

'Sometimes,' he said, 'I dream that I'm practising as a doctor and that I haven't passed my finals.'

As we finally staggered out of the restaurant back into dingy London, both of us a bit the worse for drink, I marvelled at the old sameness of Harvey and felt a surge of genuine affection towards him. For all his crookedness, for all his self-centredness, he was strangely open and naturally friendly.

About a week later I was invited to supper and set out for the short walk between our two houses with a feeling of good cheer which I hadn't begun to feel for weeks. The days were getting noticeably longer and all at once it seemed as if the end might at last be in sight. I was looking forward to seeing Harvey again, to seeing where he lived and to meeting Moira.

As I stood on the front doorstep of their house, I heard a full-throated rendering of '*E lucevan le stelle*' coming from inside. At first I supposed it to be a recording playing very loudly and then I remembered Harvey's conviction that he too could have been Caruso, Pavarotti, whoever. I smiled to myself as I rang the bell.

A tall, long-legged redhead in well-cut jeans and a huge jersey, russet like her hair, who looked almost young enough to be Harvey's daughter, came to the door. As she opened it with her left hand, she held a cigarette and a drink together in her right hand.

'Hi,' she said. 'I'm Moira. Come on in.' She made way for me to cross the threshold and pushed the door to behind me so what with that and the drink and the cigarette, it was quite impossible to shake her hand. Instead I just stood there rather awkwardly, struggling out of my coat and wondering what to say next. For some reason, despite anything Harvey might have said about Moira, I was quite unprepared for the reality of her. I don't in fact think that he can have told me quite how young she was. She must have been in her early thirties. I immediately noticed a large solitaire diamond loosely worn on her ring finger, as if casually announcing some sort of social superiority.

'*O! dolci baci, o languide carezze . . .*' Harvey was bellowing from somewhere inside. In fact he was in the kitchen cooking the supper, a ludicrous plastic apron adorned with pictures of pink smiling pigs barely covering the middle of his large body. Cooking was something that Harvey had only recently taken to and he adored it, he said. Indeed he gave us a very good supper but I felt sorry for whoever had to clear up the mess he left behind him. Moira, I initially supposed.

But it was not just the kitchen. From the moment I stepped through that front door the whole house gave me an uncomfortable feeling. Moira said they had been there for five years and yet it gave the impression of having only just been moved into. There was a packing case full of books in the front hall and the furniture in the sitting room looked as if it had been dumped there by the removal men that morning – with a 'Where would you like this settee, madam?' as they strained, sweating, to keep it aloft, waiting for madam's hurried decision.

We ate in the kitchen, surrounded by a mountain of dirty dishes and pans, and moved to the sitting room afterwards – for greater comfort, according to Harvey: but with old shoes and box files and untidily folded curtains occupying most of the seats, it was hardly an improvement. Just visible among the chaos were a few pretty pieces of furniture and one or two ornaments which I remembered from Shackles and which made me feel that I was in a dream, dreaming of somewhere that was not quite the place it was supposed to be.

Moira, I noticed, hardly ate any of Harvey's deliciously prepared supper, but smoked Silk Cut and drank white wine throughout the meal. When we left the kitchen to go to the sitting room she took two bottles with her, one of which was nearly empty and a full, newly uncorked one, holding them together at her side by their necks, a glass and the inevitable cigarette in her bejewelled other hand.

During most of supper Harvey had been talking – about opera at first and how he would have liked to have been a singer, then about cricket – all his dashed ambitions – and then about his parrots. Moira was thrilled about the idea of breeding parrots, he said.

I glanced at Moira. Her face was blank; if anything it bore a faraway look. She refilled her glass. 'I only ever drink white wine,' she said, addressing no one in particular and as if that pronouncement were in itself a declaration of absolute sobriety at all times and probity in all things.

Harvey said fatuously, 'Darling, you're beautiful,' and went on talking about the life expectancy of the hyacinth macaw. I noticed that at regular intervals throughout the evening he interrupted his garrulous flow to address some banal compliment to his wife. Since Moira never reacted, it was almost as if he were merely telling me to notice how young and pretty she was. Perhaps I was supposed to congratulate him.

I tried to ask Moira about herself and her child, who was already in bed by the time I arrived, but to little effect. She is a woman who is quite incapable of concentrating on what anyone else is saying for a single moment. She looks at times, when you speak to her, like a person attempting desperately to comprehend a foreign language of which he or she has only the barest smattering. Occasionally she will look you straight in the eye, staring almost rudely as if seeing right through you, and, for a moment, you may be fooled into thinking that she is listening, although it very soon becomes apparent that her mind is somewhere quite else, for no sooner have you finished speaking than she will say something emphatic in portentous tones – something totally irrelevant, generally something about herself. She will make a remark about her hair or perhaps her hairdresser, about her weight, her inability to sleep or she will complain about one of the many injustices that life has seen fit to deal out to her.

'Van Oosten,' she suddenly said, topping up her glass once more, and referring by his surname, as I later discovered, to her first husband, 'is a self-made man, and mean with it.'

Then she started incoherently to recount some unkindness involving money done to her by the said Van Oosten. In the middle of her rigmarole she stopped suddenly, glared at me and quite gratuitously accused me of having taken Van Oosten's side. I had said nothing but was quietly trying to imagine how Harvey and Moira managed to coexist at all, and I was also beginning to wonder how Moira had managed to remain upright on the ski slopes the week before. If indeed she had.

I looked at Harvey; perhaps he too had taken seriously to the bottle over the last years. He appeared to be quite oblivious to anything that had been said about Van Oosten, having himself moved on from macaws to cockatiels, about which he was pontificating. He didn't seem drunk, but then Harvey is a big man with a strong head who has always been able to hold his drink comparatively well.

It was time I left, I felt, but when I looked at my watch it was ridiculously early. I decided that I would have to stay for at least another half-hour, listening to this unbearable confluence of nonsense from both sides of my head.

Moira had begun talking about all the important people she had met when she was married to Van Oosten. Inventing, like Harvey, for all I know. Yes, yes, yes, of course she knew the Home Secretary and this writer and that actor and this grandee and that poet laureate – they'd all come to some terrifically grand house the Van Oostens owned in Surrey or Kent. I felt my head would burst if I had to hear any more of this rubbish, which had a particularly distressing quality in that there appeared to be a corollary between the way Moira didn't listen and the way she spoke. Having not listened, it was as if she failed to understand the need for that function and therefore did not require to be listened to. She was talking, in effect, to herself.

At last the time had come when I could leave with decency, saying untruthfully that I had an early start the following day. Harvey leaped to his feet to see me out, apparently unembarrassed by his wife whom, as she staggered to her feet, he once again described as beautiful.

We went to the door together, myself exclaiming somewhat gauchely on the pleasantness of the evening. I was just putting on my coat when I was startled by a blood-curdling cry from upstairs which developed into a long, mournful wail.

'What on earth . . . ?' I wanted to know.

'It's Frederick,' Harvey said. 'Sleepwalking . . .' He turned to go to his child and I felt a pang of pity for him as I watched his back view disappearing up the stairs two at a time.

There was no reaction at all from Moira, who might as well not have heard her son's cry. She opened the door to let me out and as she did so, she looked hard at me with the exaggerated concentration of a drunk and asked, 'Who did you say you were?'

Walking home, I naturally pondered on what had become of Harvey, a man in his mid-fifties, banging on about parrots, living in shambles, doing the cooking, running after his child. It all seemed very odd. It certainly wasn't quite the Harvey I knew and I couldn't help wondering how and why he'd managed to get himself into such a situation. Surely not just for Van Oosten's money.

Chapter IX

Later I learned more about what had been happening to Harvey during all those years in which I hadn't seen him. I even met his second wife – not entirely by chance, I have to admit.

In the spring, after that first dreadful winter at last came to an end, I went to stay with my sister who is married to an estate agent in the West Country. I hadn't seen her since my return to England and was feeling rather bad about endlessly putting off visiting her, but, having never really got on with her husband, who is a dull, smug fellow, I'd been tempted to make excuses. But I had no desire to hurt the feelings of a sister for whom, although she is much older than I, and despite the fact that our lives have taken such different paths, I have a genuine affection.

Expecting nothing more than a family weekend with a good walk on Exmoor perhaps, I took the train on Friday evening to Taunton. It arrived half an hour late, in the rain, but my brother-in-law was there at the station, pacing up and down the platform, fuming at what he no doubt regarded as British incompetence and at the typical inefficiency of British

Rail. He welcomed me with too firm a handshake, almost crushing my fingers in his iron grip, and told me that my sister had not come to the station because she was preparing a feast for the prodigal. She never made such a fuss over her poor, hard-working husband.

It took a good three-quarters of an hour, driving through blinding rain, to get back to the Somerset longhouse – a low, white-painted, slate-roofed farmhouse – which was their home and which, as I was to discover in the bright light of the following morning, looked down across a narrow valley to a steep green hill dotted with sheep and gambolling woolly lambs. How much nicer a place than the poky little town house where they lived when I had last visited them so many years before.

A rough track led from the house to a lane that wound its way along the valley between high hedgerows, beyond which a stream, bordered by the occasional stunted tree, trickled through lush meadows. It was very, very green; brilliantly luminous after the rain and, gazing at it out of the window, I was filled with a great sense of peace. Certainly Harvey and his problems were never further from my mind, so I was quite surprised when my sister asked me at breakfast if I had seen him lately. She remembered Harvey from years gone by, but mostly she only knew him by repute – Harvey being someone about whom everyone talked, of course.

All the same, I wondered at her suddenly asking after him, until she explained that his second wife had become a great friend of hers and would be coming to supper that evening.

We made the usual remarks about the world being a small place, but what really interested me was anything she could tell me about Harvey during what I thought of as the 'intervening years'. Naturally I was fascinated by the prospect of meeting the second wife. I said that I had seen Harvey in

London and I remember, as we sat around the breakfast table, describing his life with Moira at length and in the vividest of terms.

Not surprisingly, nothing came to light about Harvey that reflected much to his credit.

He'd been on the loose in London for several years before he met Penelope. It was at the time of the picture gallery when he was running all over the place with Zed in tow. After he sold the gallery he tried his hand at various enterprises, most of which turned out disastrously, but for each of which he developed, however fleetingly, an enormous, wild enthusiasm. There had been the glass-blowing episode, the wine-importing business in which he burned his fingers badly, the bucket-shop travel agency and so forth. I doubt that Harvey himself would be able to remember all the different concerns in which he has been involved over the years, not all of them by any means catastrophic, but then Harvey, when something is going well, has a way of growing quickly bored. In fact, the picture gallery was probably the most successful of all his ventures and might even have continued to be so had it been run on slightly more honest lines. He must have rued the day that he allowed Zed to make off with all those Cornish paintings, to sell them only a few years later for large sums of money. But Harvey is never one to look back. The concept of regret is most probably unknown to him.

Who knows why Harvey decided to marry Penelope? I should think she must sometimes have wondered herself. He'd had a lot of different women since Frances and had shown no sign of wanting to marry any of them. He seemed at the time to be not only a confirmed bachelor, but a bad marriage prospect to boot with a dicey reputation for business and an equally bad reputation for his treatment of women. I can only think that he married Penelope in much the same spirit that he married Deirdre.

Harvey was most likely bored when he married Penelope, wanting excitement of some kind – a change, wanting to draw attention to himself, thinking a party would be fun. Someone once suggested that Harvey in fact married Penelope for money; not for her money, however, but for his own. At the time he was certainly running into quite serious financial difficulties and there was, everyone knew, some family trust which he had been trying to break for a while, seeing it as the only sure way out of his troubles. Marriage might well prove to be the one thing which would persuade the trustees to change their minds. I don't know what happened in fact, but despite all his wild undertakings, Harvey has never seemed to be particularly short of cash.

When he married Penelope they bought a red sandstone manor house in a village near Taunton – a plain house apparently, but with fine views over the Quantocks. So Harvey finally achieved his boyhood dream of settling in the West Country, although settling is hardly the word to describe what he did. To begin with he was between jobs – or enterprises – so that when he went to Somerset he needed to find an occupation. The first thing he thought of was – clever old Harvey – cider, and from that he moved on to applejack brandy. He had a couple of orchards around the house but no knowledge whatsoever of the old art of cider-making. He set up a press in a barn and an illegal still in the cellar and to begin with things went remarkably well. With his aptitude for picking up information quite quickly, he managed to get the cider-making on its feet within a couple of years, even managing to find a little corner in the market.

But it was the still in the cellar that really captured Harvey's imagination; he saw himself as producing an exquisite liqueur to rival the finest of old calvados. While it was only in its untamed infancy, a considerable amount of effort went into fantasizing about what he would call this magical, as yet illegal product. In fact it never survived beyond its infancy, as, for all his success with the cider, Harvey was never able to grasp the secret of the magic formula which would turn his harsh, sour, watery substance into something worth bottling, let alone labelling.

After a few years, it seemed to Harvey that the cider-making could more or less look after itself with Penelope – who already had two babies – to replace him as supervisor. He had probably lost faith in the still, was surely impatient with the ties inflicted by a family and bored with living in the country. He began to go away more and more often: at first to Normandy to investigate the calvados industry, as he claimed, although there were rumours at the time that it was not so much the calvados industry as the presence in Rouen of a French PR girl with a husky voice who bore a close resemblance to the young Brigitte Bardot that attracted him back and back across the Channel.

Poor Penelope had a struggle to keep going. She coped manfully with the cider-making, although she felt betrayed and let down by Harvey, who showed little concern for her and who generally complained about spending any money at all on the house, the heating, the children's clothes, even the grocery bills, and who was never there when most needed.

Harvey is one of those men who give the false impression of being generous; who spend what they want on their own pleasures, which not infrequently include entertaining their friends, but who cannot bear to see money spent on anything which does not bring themselves immediate satisfaction.

At Shackles in those early days, he'd wanted a lush, pretty

little house; it suited the image he had of himself then and presented the desired picture of the sort of person he wanted to be to the world. Later, with money a little tighter and Harvey himself hardened, he took to enquiring why the children needed new shoes, to complaining when Penelope was on the telephone and to refusing to buy gin for her occasional gin and tonic, since whisky was his tipple. Whatever economies were made, they never seemed directly to affect Harvey, who continued to dash off to London to order expensive new suits from his tailor and who went backwards and forwards to France as if he hadn't a care in the world.

The red sandstone house began to look as if it had seen better days and Penelope began to look older than her years and tired. It was at around this time that my sister first met her at the house of a mutual friend, although the two didn't make friends until after Penelope's marriage had finally collapsed. My sister was initially amazed that this should be Harvey's wife – this grey, downtrodden-looking person who seemed barely able to smile and whose face was permanently pinched into an expression of distracted anxiety. It seemed hardly surprising if Harvey made his excuses and escaped from time to time.

Eventually the still ground to a halt and so presumably did the Bardot look-alike as Harvey gave up any pretence of making calvados. The cider business was by this time limping along as, with Harvey absent and Penelope occupied with her children, it had not had the concentrated attention it required. Between them Penelope and Harvey had failed to see the opportunities which were open to them, they had not expanded where they should have done, had cruised along until they began to lose customers and were eventually obliged to close the business. Harvey, naturally, blamed the economic climate of the times for this failure, appeared almost to laugh it off with a wave of the hand and began to look about for something else to amuse him.

What he immediately found was the German au pair girl. So Harvey was back in Somerset for a while on a more or less permanent basis, but it must have been cold comfort to Penelope to know that what attracted him there was not so much she or her children as Gudrun. Harvey, it appears, made little if any attempt to disguise his passion for the girl, which she in turn, bored by English children, the English countryside and uninterested in her English classes, was briefly prepared to reciprocate. How she excused her behaviour towards Penelope is not recorded.

But what my sister learned later from Penelope was that no sooner had Gudrun returned to Hamburg than she wrote to Harvey, telling him that she was pregnant, that he was the father of her child, and asking him for money.

Harvey of course swore that he had never slept with the girl and then gave the game away by saying, 'Anyway, it's only her word against mine.' He seemed blissfully to suppose that given a choice no one in their right senses would believe Gudrun rather than him. There was quite a lot of trouble after that but luckily for Harvey it eventually turned out that the girl was lying anyway, that she wasn't pregnant at all, but had just been trying it on. So perhaps Harvey was right about no one being prepared to believe her. It takes one to know one, so they say.

As soon as that little problem had blown over, Harvey was on the move again, ceaselessly, restlessly looking for something to do, for a role in which he could at last feel comfortable. At one point he started to write a thriller with the avowed intention of it becoming a blockbuster. He felt he'd had a varied and interesting enough life to have the material to pull it off, but that didn't prevent him from having to fly away all over the world for purposes of research. It was Berlin one week, Bangkok the next, Kenya in February and still the manuscript didn't appear to advance.

I can well imagine Harvey in his new-found role as a writer, suddenly dressed in a worn corduroy jacket, a red spotted cravat tied at his throat, hair – once so neatly brushed – ruffled in imitation of Beethoven, the proverbial artist. He must have been most annoying, talking and talking and talking about his unplanned plot, about the art of writing and about how his book would certainly be made into a major feature film. It would have all the ingredients: white slavery in the Golden Triangle, drug barons in Chiang Mai, a Polish countess scaling the Berlin Wall, big-game poaching in Kenya – there was to be no end to it. And the hero would be an English cricketer of the old-fashioned Bedser twins variety, Brylcreemed hair, baggy flannels and all.

But there was one thing which did keep Harvey at home for most of the summer months throughout those years and that was cricket. Almost as soon as he'd bought the red sandstone house, he organized a village cricket team whose fixtures continued to take pride of place in his diary. Funnily enough Harvey – who, as I have said, is never a man for regrets – mentioned that cricket team when I saw him in London. He'd had enough of living in the country, he said. Then, with his head on one side as for a moment a slightly mournful expression crossed his face, he'd added, 'But I miss the cricket.' A rare moment of truth perhaps.

Harvey's skill at cricket and courage on the field earned him considerable respect locally and my sister told me that Penelope, long after the separation and after years of what must have been a very lonely marriage, still boasted of Harvey's prowess, of how he always went in first before the younger men, to take the brunt of the fast bowlers –

something like that. Perhaps Penelope needed an idea to cling to as a kind of explanation for why she had married Harvey in the first place. Harvey who was, after all, the father of her children.

The novel of course was never written and after a while Harvey shed the spotted cravat and began to brush his hair again. It was probably around then that he took to fishing. A most unlikely sport for Harvey, whom it is difficult to imagine standing patiently and silently for hours on the river bank. I shall certainly never forget my brief glimpse of him that time when he was in his fishing phase. I was back in England on holiday one summer and was totally taken by surprise when I saw him all kitted up. And come to think of it, he himself may have even been a little embarrassed to see me so unexpectedly. We hadn't met for several years and he could hardly have known that I would be staying with mutual friends on whom he happened to call.

In a strange way, habitual liars are often believed even by the people who know them best, presumably because generally speaking most of us are used to believing what we are told by friends without question. So a man like Harvey can weave a fantastic tale and be believed by a lot of the people a lot of the time although eventually what he says will inevitably be taken with a pinch of salt by anyone with a grain of sense. I recognize that even I, who have known him for so many years, can occasionally find myself absorbed by something he is saying, completely taken in by total nonsense, convinced by his emphatic assertions that he is telling the truth, until suddenly he goes right over the top or contradicts himself or begins to stammer a bit too nervously. Then I remind myself to watch it. This is Harvey.

Of course one always wonders quite how much he deceives

himself. I rather suspect that the extent to which he does so is in precisely inverse proportion to the extent to which he deceives others. As they register disbelief, so he increasingly attempts to convince them of the truth of what he is saying, but instead succeeds only in convincing himself while driving his listeners to greater degrees of scepticism.

In any case, according to my sister's account which came from Penelope, Harvey eventually tried to get a divorce on the grounds of his wife's unreasonable behaviour. He seems to have imagined that that way he might have been able to avoid giving her so much money. Harvey's restlessly fertile imagination was stretched to the utmost in order to conjure up extremes of unreasonable behaviour of which Penelope might have been guilty. In the end, after it was over, Penelope was able to see the funny side of it all. Harvey must have been in his element.

He told his solicitor that Penelope, from the earliest days of their marriage, had insisted on sleeping with her giant poodle beside her in the bed, that she had refused to seek a remedy for a particularly virulent form of athlete's foot to which she was prone, that she refused to supervise the business while he was away, that she insisted on keeping all the windows open throughout the bitterest winter weather, that by feeding them on jam she encouraged bats to hibernate in the house and that she would never entertain his friends. All this and much more.

How could Penelope prove that she had never had the slightest sign of athlete's foot since she was at school and long before she had ever even heard of Harvey? But equally, what chance had Harvey of making all this nonsense stick? Eventually his lawyers must have become fed up – although not before billing him for vast amounts of money – because

Harvey withdrew the complaints and no more was ever heard about bats and jam and poodles and icy rooms. In the end, it was Penelope who turned the whole thing into a funny story.

Harvey to this day probably believes that most of what he invented was true.

When Penelope arrived that evening for supper, I was initially surprised by her appearance. She was not at all as I would have imagined a wife of Harvey's, although, given the unlikely combination of Deirdre and Moira, I don't know that I had any right to expect anything.

Funnily enough Penelope reminded me rather of Deirdre's bossy sister Marion: tall, with clear-cut features, a country lady – what might be called 'doggy', with tweed skirts and sensible shoes. I could almost imagine her allowing a giant poodle to climb into bed beside her. Of course when you meet someone who resembles someone else, it is practically impossible not to lend the characteristics of the one to the other. The more I talked to Penelope, the more difficult I found it to reconcile the personality that emerged with what seemed to be Marion's outward appearance. I have never particularly taken to Marion, who, although perfectly pleasant, is an unimaginative, didactic woman, but Harvey, I seemed to remember, had absolutely loathed her. I couldn't help wondering if he ever noticed the physical resemblance between her and his second wife.

Penelope kept one Pekingese – no giant poodle – and a pony for her children; but the pony was small and old and the children had more or less grown out of it so it lived in a field, to all intents and purposes retired, threatening laminitis every spring. Penelope's passion was her garden. She loved to be in it, but unlike Marion, she was an educated woman, widely read and with an intelligent interest in a variety of subjects. She was frank, but diffident and humorous. Much too good for Harvey, I thought.

At first I had no intention of talking about Harvey but Penelope immediately raised the subject, saying that she had heard from my sister that I had known him for a long time. She was curious to hear about his new wife, wondering affectionately, I thought, how he was. She seemed to think that he had now reached some kind of watershed in his life whereby – partly because of everything that had gone before and partly because of his age – things were beginning really to go against him. It was becoming more and more difficult for him to pick up the pieces and run with them. He had lost so much credibility.

This certainly seemed to be borne out by what I had seen of him and Moira, although, of course, his manner had been as ebullient as ever. But years ago none of us would ever have imagined Harvey closeted with a hopeless drunk, cooking for her, washing up no doubt, running after the baby.

Penelope smiled wryly at the idea. It wouldn't hurt Harvey, she said, to have to think about someone else for a change, but she couldn't honestly see it lasting. What would happen to him then? However badly things had turned out for Harvey in the past, he always managed to shrug them off and rise on the crest of the next incoming wave, but by now she was beginning to wonder whether there was another wave on the horizon to carry him buoyantly back to the shore.

Harvey, Penelope said, was quite incapable of being on his own, even for an evening. If he was alone for ten minutes he would pick up the telephone to ring anyone: this person, that person, talk, talk, talk. He'd ring Australia as easily as he'd ring London, at any time of day or night, to ask the score of the test match or what the weather was like on the third day of play. Penelope found all that difficult to understand since, having spent a great deal of time on her own – she was indeed alone now with the children away at school – she had reached the conclusion that she would certainly rather remain alone than tie herself to someone just for the sake of company.

I looked at her and sensed an inner calm; I thought that she herself would make a good companion and wondered if she would ever think of marrying again or whether the experience with Harvey had been enough to put her off the idea for good.

Another thing was, Penelope told me, that Harvey was not nearly as well off as he had been, which was something that he would find very difficult to adapt to. Harvey was spoilt and had become accustomed to having his own way, to spending money like water and to presuming that when things became difficult there would always be some miraculously untapped source on which he could draw to get himself out of trouble. They had lost a certain amount of money over the cider, which was hardly surprising as Harvey was never there, always trotting off to France and leaving her to take charge whilst never giving her a free hand to make decisions. It had been a nightmare and Penelope was heartily relieved when the whole thing folded.

'What's he into now?' she enquired with a laugh.

'Breeding parrots,' I said.

She laughed again. Harvey, she opined, was a fascinating person. Someone about whom people could and did talk endlessly but about whom they never really came to any conclusions. The most peculiar thing was that, however badly he behaved, everyone always ended up, if not forgiving him, at least feeling some kind of indulgence towards him.

'After all,' she said, 'even I don't wish him ill, but he'll go to his grave lying, with half the people still believing half of what he says half the time.'

By the time we'd reached the pudding course, my sister suggested that there really must be something for us to talk about other than Harvey. My brother-in-law, who had hardly joined in, who clearly found the whole topic distasteful and who disapproved of Harvey anyway, was looking superior and petulant, so, to please him, we obediently began to talk of different things like the weather or the monarchy.

Before she left, Penelope asked when I would be returning to London and when I told her I would be going after lunch the following day, she invited me to come for tea or a drink on the way to the station. My sister, who planned to take me to the station, seemed pleased by the idea and agreed that we would look in.

So it was that I was able to see the house which had been Harvey's home for longer than anywhere else since he'd left the parental lodge in Scotland.

It is a plain, red sandstone manor house which sits rather grandly on a small hill behind a high stone wall, looking out over fields and hills towards the sea, across the village clustered beneath it – a mixture of old and dainty new – and across the village cricket ground, with its rickety white-painted pavilion where, according to Penelope, Harvey was still missed. Somewhere on the edge of the village, counterbalancing a thirteenth-century church tower to the left, there rises the shining space-age edifice of a silo; its rounded top that day reflected the last rays of the afternoon sun.

As we stood in the garden, bright with daffodils, bursting with the promise of lilac and choisya, and sweet smelling of daphne, I thought of Harvey in this lovely place, of how he had inevitably grown bored here, and I felt sad for him.

Penelope pointed at the shimmering silo. 'We were

appalled when they put that up,' she said. 'But now I've almost grown to love it. If you look at it for long enough and think about it, you can imbue it with a certain beauty of its own. It's the best you can do.'

We went into the house for a cup of tea. It was quite unlike Shackles or, for that matter, Harvey's house in London. It was the kind of house that the real Harvey – if there is any such thing – would probably have liked or even dreamed of. I could see him striding about on his long legs, relaxed, imagining he fitted the picture, proud of the house, of the view, complaining about the silo. Inside it was quite untidy, pretty, an unaffected sort of house with everywhere evidence of family life: tennis rackets in the hall, bunches of daffodils and pussy willow stuck hurriedly into jugs, dog baskets in the kitchen, books and papers on every table, seed catalogues lying about, old-fashioned comfort in the sitting room, soft colours, faded curtains, dusty rosettes – presumably won by children at gymkhanas – on the dresser in the kitchen. When I visited the downstairs lavatory before leaving, I even noticed, hanging on the wall, a framed photograph of Harvey in whites with what must have been his cricket team all lined up, poker-faced, in front of the village pavilion. I felt strangely hurt for Harvey, obliged to leave such a home; but then it had been his choice, although one that he might not have made were he not eternally the victim of his own lies.

I wondered what his relationship with Penelope had been at its best. It was difficult to imagine them together, but she seemed strong, sensible, warm-hearted, perhaps the kind of person who might have been able to cope with him, to forgive him and to accept him as he was. But why should anyone ultimately be expected to build their life round another person's mythomania? Is it even possible, without losing one's own integrity and joining in the game? Penelope was probably much better off without Harvey.

As we drank our tea and ate sponge cake, Penelope suddenly laughed. 'It's funny your being here,' she said. 'And I'm so glad to have met you because Harvey used to talk about you an awful lot, you know. But I somehow imagined you quite differently. I'm sure Harvey said you had red hair.'

'Harvey,' I said, 'is quite incapable of telling the truth.'

My sister was stirring a sweetener into her tea. 'There you go again,' she said. 'You can't leave the subject alone – what is it about Harvey?'

'Well, for one thing,' Penelope volunteered, 'I have been on my own for several years now and yet hardly a day goes by without it dawning on me that something – something quite unimportant which I accepted unquestioningly as gospel truth – is just another of Harvey's lies. However well you know someone, however aware you are of the fact that they lie, you still go on believing them. We are not programmed to mistrust a person who says that X has red hair or that it's only fifteen miles from here to Wincanton. Harvey could sit there,' she pointed across the table at me, 'and tell you that it had rained all morning and, although you might have spent the morning gardening with a blue sky over your head, it wouldn't – unless you were really concentrating – occur to you to disbelieve him.'

'A lot of people see Harvey not really as a liar, but as someone who exaggerates or tells stories to entertain,' I said, to placate her.

'Huh!' She tossed her head. 'If it were just that! Harvey's only understanding of the truth is as something to be avoided at all costs. He wouldn't bother me any more except that I worry about the children. Of course they believe what he says and of course they want to . . .'

At that moment the telephone rang. Penelope left the table to answer it. I heard her tone change to one of concern after the first 'Hello' and, supposing her to be speaking to one of her children, I deemed the moment to be right for me to go in search of the downstairs lavatory. My sister picked up an old copy of *Spectator* which happened to be lying on the kitchen table and appeared to be absorbed by it.

When I got back Penelope was just putting down the telephone.

'There you are,' she said. 'That's Harvey all over – poor Catherine is in floods of tears and I don't blame her. If you lie the way he does – and has done all his life – I don't believe you notice you're doing it any more. You certainly do it without a qualm, even to your own children.'

What had happened, it seemed, was that Catherine had been supposed to go to London to stay with her father for the weekend but Harvey had rung the school on the Friday morning to say that he and Moira and the baby all had flu and that the weekend would be a dreary one for her, so she had better stay at school. She could of course have gone to her mother instead, but at the time she didn't want to let Harvey down by admitting that he had let her down, although she was pretty annoyed with him for having flu. So she'd said nothing to Penelope, which was silly, Penelope thought, because of course the truth was bound to come out in the end.

So Catherine had spent a gloomy weekend at school, no doubt feeling very sorry for herself, and then, on Sunday afternoon, another girl, who had been home for the weekend, came bounding up to Catherine, saying, 'I met your dad last night.'

Of course Catherine had denied that any such thing was

possible but, alas, had eventually been persuaded that it was true.

'He was brilliant,' this other girl had said, just as Catherine burst into tears and stormed away.

'Can you imagine a more callow lie to be told by a supposedly mature man?' Penelope was clearly distressed.

It was time then for us to be going if I was to catch my train, so we thanked Penelope, wished her goodbye and I hoped – sincerely – to meet her again. It wasn't until some time later that I learned from my sister what had really happened that weekend.

Moira, it appears, had had a cold and was probably making heavy weather about it – perhaps she was drinking even more than usual – and Harvey was no doubt getting pretty fed up in his role as mother and housekeeper. Perhaps he would have been pleased to see Catherine, of whom he is said to be genuinely fond and whose presence would have broken the monotony of his existence in Notting Hill, if an old friend had not rung him quite out of the blue on the Thursday night.

That friend was Zed. After all those years – Zed! Zed with his usual optimism – and perhaps a certain insight into character – was convinced that Harvey would have forgiven and forgotten whatever had passed between them before. Zed had a brilliant idea up his sleeve which he was sure would interest Harvey.

He was in the import-export business now and he had this friend down in Cornwall with whom he was trying to set up a company: what about Harvey joining them on Saturday for the weekend to discuss whether he might be interested in going in with the two of them? If he was interested, it would mean a trip to Amsterdam and Copenhagen the following week. Was Harvey free? Harvey was of course suddenly as free as a bird and instantly ready to forget about parrots.

The Cornish friend unfortunately turned out to have a daughter at the same school as Catherine; she was at home for the weekend and it was she therefore who spilled the beans to Catherine.

Not long after that Zed was arrested and charged with importing obscene material into this country. Eventually he went down for something like eighteen months. No one ever discovered quite how much, if at all, Harvey was implicated in the whole affair, about which he, not surprisingly, claims complete ignorance. Zed had been talking to him about another matter entirely, which is strange since the Cornish character also went to prison for the same offence, although his sentence was considerably lighter than Zed's.

Some people even remember Harvey setting out for Copenhagen at around that time, apparently on some mission for Zed; but Harvey flatly denies ever having set foot in D-d-denmark.

Chapter X

With the winter behind me and spring in the air I began to settle more easily into my new London routine. I picked up with old friends, found a reasonable job and life took off again, so that before very long the years I had spent abroad – and even my marriage – seemed to have become part of a dream or at least of another existence from which I had grown strangely detached. Occasionally the smell of spices issuing out of an Indian restaurant as I passed awoke painful, bitter-sweet memories causing me to hasten my step; or, if I happened to be up early, in the dawn light I would hear the call of the east.

Among the friends whom I saw not infrequently were both Deirdre and Harvey. Harvey, I have to admit, I had come to dread seeing, but then there he was, just round the corner from me, ringing me up from time to time, almost begging me to come for supper or to meet him for a drink. There is no doubt about it that Harvey had at last fallen on hard times, not only because he was running out of funds, but because most of his friends had given up seeing him. He and Moira were, not surprisingly, rarely asked out; they lived together in squalor, bickering most of the time. Their child, who was not particularly attractive at its best, sensing the general disregard in which it was held by its parents, did everything tiresome it could think of to attract attention to itself so that, as it grew older, it grew more and more difficult.

Harvey's usual good nature and inborn *bonhomie* prevented him from self-pity or indeed from ever admitting that anything was particularly wrong, but there was now, I noticed, a shifty, darting look which had not been there before. And sometimes, fleetingly, the scared, uncomprehending look of a cornered animal. But still he appeared young, almost as though he were untouched by life, and still he sang arias from *Don Giovanni* or bellowed out old favourites like 'Red Sails in the Sunset' or 'Old Man River'. The truth is that I felt sorry for him.

Since the most recent fiasco with Zed some of the stuffing seemed to have been knocked out of Harvey. Whether what had happened had frightened him or not, I have no means of telling but certainly, for a while at least, his fervid imagination appeared to dry up so that he had no idea in which direction to turn his talents. I suppose he had a little money left to live on and then Moira, of course, as everyone knew, was very well off.

I first met Harvey's and Penelope's son, Charlie, when he was about seventeen years old, I suppose. I had invited Harvey and Moira to supper one Saturday evening – it really was my turn. On the Saturday morning Harvey rang to say that Moira wouldn't be coming but could he instead bring his son, who was in London for half-term? I was delighted, infinitely preferring the idea of meeting Charlie to the thought of another evening with Moira becoming increasingly stupefied and increasingly aggressive. Not that Harvey himself was particularly sober of late. In fact, glass for glass I doubt that he was far behind Moira, but then, as I have said, he was better able to hold his drink. I was pretty sure that Harvey, too, preferred the idea of an evening without Moira.

When I opened the door to Harvey and Charlie, I almost wanted to laugh. Charlie so resembled his father as a young man that it seemed uncanny. I searched his features for any likeness to his mother but could perceive none, although I hoped for his sake that he had inherited some of her character. I could hardly bear the thought of another Harvey.

In fact the evening turned out to be rather an awkward one with Charlie sitting gauchely in the corner, smoking roll-ups, saying not very much although answering quite agreeably when addressed. He told me that he was in the school first eleven, told me what A levels he was taking, told me that he planned to go to India or Thailand in his gap year, but volunteered very little of his own accord. India or Thailand, it didn't seem to matter which. He may well have felt ill at ease between his father and me, but he showed none of his father's spark of originality nor any of his panache. When questioned about why he wanted to go to India or Thailand, he could find very little to say. Despite being at a reputable public school, he seemed to think that Bombay was the capital of India and had never heard of Partition. India and Thailand were for him, I think, just places where people with backpacks went after school, probably to smoke dope or even to try something more exciting, certainly without having given much thought to their destination or to the irrelevance of their own expedition.

Perhaps I was beginning to feel old, but I couldn't help being somewhat irritated by Charlie and his general gormlessness. In my mind I compared him to Deirdre's son, Will, the only other person I knew of that age, and suddenly remembered that the two boys were at school together. I had always thought that Will, with the laces of his trainers untied and permanent music plugged into his ears, appeared somewhat lackadaisical; his mother certainly complained that he did no work at school. But as I had grown to know Will better, I had become fond of him. Behind his teenage indolence there lay a warm heart and a decent approach to life. Perhaps Charlie was the same.

Harvey was talking about cars. He had decided that if Charlie passed his A levels, he would buy him a car. Charlie seemed to think that this was perfectly in order and neither father nor son questioned the quality of the pass. Would a few Es be worthy of a rusty jalopy while the shiny Mazda after which Charlie hankered could be his for a row of As? I wondered, and secretly thought it would do the lad good to walk.

I was tired by the time they left and I closed the front door on them with a certain relief, turning my mind instantly to other matters.

It wasn't until later on that summer, after the A levels had been sat, that I even thought about Charlie again. It was Deirdre who spoke of him with a certain amount of anxiety on account of the fact that Will had suddenly announced his intention of accompanying Charlie to India.

Until then Will had refused to consider what he would do during his gap year. Perhaps he was secretly terrified that the gap would eventually prove to be more than a gap since his inability to apply himself to his studies made it increasingly unlikely that he would achieve the grades required for him to go to university. Then perhaps India presented itself as a way out of trouble. Like a dog lowering its tail and cringing in an attempt to make itself invisible when in disgrace, Will, who was intelligent and capable of doing well in his exams, probably felt that it would be politic to shrink away to nothing and not be seen for a while.

What particularly surprised Deirdre was that Will, unlike so many young people these days, had never shown the slightest interest in foreign travel; he had as a younger boy – before the Walkman took over – been interested in sport and scientific experiment, inventing gadgets. Deirdre knew about Charlie, of course, but she had never met him and certainly disliked the idea of having to have anything to do with Harvey or even Penelope, but she obviously wanted to know what plans the young people had in mind. Anything she had heard from Will seemed remarkably woolly and she was, not surprisingly, curious to know more about Charlie. She was half glad that Will had decided to do something but, at the same time, she fervently wished that he could have found any companion other than Harvey's son with whom to travel.

In the event neither boy did very well in his exams but Charlie, who had not yet even passed his driving test, was still hoping to get his car. The two shook the dust of school off their feet with sighs of relief and disappeared together to Somerset to play cricket with Harvey's old village team.

Deirdre was both irritated and embarrassed by the whole scenario, but she was busy at the hospital and besides could not really see that there was any good reason why the boys should not be friends.

From about this time Charlie and Will became almost inseparable and eventually Charlie was brought to the cottage in Berkshire, where I happened to be staying at the time. If I was struck by Charlie's resemblance to his father, it is hard to imagine how Deirdre felt when she first saw him. She did tell me later that it was quite a shock, particularly since she hadn't seen Harvey for so many years that, whereas I had seen him change gradually with time and knew him as a middle-aged man, she could only remember him as he had been, without a grey hair or a line on his face. When Charlie walked through the door it was for her as if Harvey had suddenly walked straight back into her life; perhaps again, rather like one of those dreams in which none of the people are quite who they are meant to be and none of the places are quite as they should be.

After the initial shock of seeing Charlie, Deirdre gradually warmed to him. He wasn't a bad boy, she said, the two would do all right travelling together. Perhaps she was just comforting herself, since, as far as I could see, there was nothing very much to recommend the trip for either boy, mainly because they appeared to have very little motivation. I longed to hear them evince some enthusiasm for where they were going rather than for the tapes they were going to take with them to block their ears and minds to all that lay around them.

I tried to tell them a little from my own experience of those parts of the world, but they listened politely before going on to compare makes of backpack and prices of round-the-world tickets, depending on whether you were stopping off at Sydney or Bangkok. It seemed as though neither of them cared in the least where they went, so long as they went somewhere. They might have landed on the moon or in Patagonia with equal lack of amazement. I'm sure this worried Deirdre but there was nothing she could do about it except hope that when they landed in Bombay they would be jolted out of their torpor.

Harvey, not surprisingly, was far less concerned than Deirdre was about the trip, in fact he seemed, if anything, to be vicariously excited. He would have liked to be in Will's and Charlie's shoes; he wished that such opportunities had been open to young people in his day. God knows what he would have made of them! As it was, he could hardly leave the subject alone and on a couple of occasions when I saw him he mentioned the possibility of his flying out to join the boys for a while when they reached Bangkok. I muttered something about wondering whether that was a good idea but Harvey didn't listen. He was determined that by the time they had been to India and Nepal, bumming around for three or four months, they would be delighted to see him in Thailand. Well, it was none of my business. I could only suppose that Harvey, being Harvey, wanted a change, a diversion, an adventure; he wanted in some blindly optimistic way to recapture his youth and he wanted, too, the kudos to be gained from playing the wise man, the mentor. That, at any rate, was what I presumed, but I could well imagine that he wanted also to get away from Moira, although it did occur to me that there was a far greater danger inherent in leaving Moira – even with a nanny – alone and drunken in charge of a child in London, than there ever was in allowing two young adults, however callow, to set off round the world together.

I spent the evening with Deirdre after she had seen Will off at Heathrow. Harvey had been there too, although Penelope had not. Deirdre hadn't wanted to see Harvey and neither had she wanted to hear the advice he was giving the two young men.

'A lot of twaddle,' she said. 'I think I need a drink,' she added, pouring whisky into a glass. 'It was a bit much waving Will off, meeting Harvey and going to work all in one day. As for Harvey,' she went on, 'he looks awful – gone to seed or something. Poor fellow, I suppose.'

Later, during supper, she came back to the subject of Harvey. 'Have you ever been into a prison?' she asked.

I definitely hadn't and neither had Ralph, which she knew,

but she had, once or twice, in her capacity as a doctor. 'Harvey, when you catch him unawares,' she said thoughtfully, 'sometimes has an expression on his face which I have only ever seen on the face of a lifer. It's difficult to explain – sort of hollow – empty and afraid.'

Harvey's reaction to seeing Deirdre was quite another matter.

'Deirdre's looking good,' he said when I next saw him. 'She's kept her looks and her figure. Perhaps I should never have left her.'

I thought of all the women – real or imagined – with whom Harvey had linked his name since leaving Deirdre and then I thought of Deirdre's quiet husband and her own successful career and I couldn't help giving a guffaw.

It was not long before Deirdre heard from Will that he and Charlie had landed safely in Bombay, that Charlie had had his money stolen and that otherwise everything was fine. After that, at irregular, intermittent intervals letters continued to arrive which not only allayed Deirdre's fears on behalf of her darling child but also led her to believe that he was enjoying the trip and – who knows – even making something of it. She felt relieved.

The two travelled up through Gujarat and Rajasthan to Delhi, where they hung around for a while before making their way on to Nepal. Then just before Christmas Will rang his parents from Kathmandu, where he said he and Charlie had both been very sick. Neither of them had eaten a thing for days – the very sight of a glass of water had made them retch. They'd lain sweating with a fever, side by side, on hard beds in a cheap hostel which smelled of drains; neither of them had ever imagined it possible to feel so ill, but the message now was not to worry, they were both feeling better, although their clothes hung loose. They were planning to set out on a trek within a couple of days and would be in the mountains over Christmas. They expected to be in Bangkok by the middle of January.

Shortly after Christmas Harvey telephoned Deirdre to say that he had booked a flight to Bangkok, where he had arranged to meet up with the boys, and was there anything Deirdre wanted him to take out to Will?

Deirdre was furious. What the hell did Harvey think he was doing? Why couldn't he leave the boys alone? They were doing fine and the last thing she could imagine them wanting was to be followed round the world by Harvey, of all people. She did actually tell him that it was a bad idea, but naturally Harvey had an answer ready. He had some business which was taking him to Bangkok. Of course he wouldn't have dreamed of going there otherwise. But it would be a shame to go and not to see Charlie and Will. Besides, they would probably welcome a square meal by now.

Deirdre didn't believe a word about Harvey having any business to do in Thailand, but she was a little worried that he might find something reprehensible in which to involve himself once he got there. He was far sillier than either of the boys and, despite his age, probably even more likely to be duped.

I don't think any of us ever heard everything about what Harvey got up to in Bangkok, where he'd been on and off before when fleeing the rigours of the Somerset winters and the monotony of family life with Penelope. But that was probably just as well. Harvey in the modern, Americanized luxury of the old Oriental Hotel, sitting on the terrace in happy hour, moist from the heat and the clinging humidity, clasping a gaudy cocktail in one sweaty hand as he gazed out across the water and swatted mosquitoes with the other, no doubt felt himself momentarily to be no less than the angels.

Joseph Conrad at least. The horror of the mighty modern city with its roaring traffic and relentless criss-crossing of highways certainly didn't impinge on him whilst he sat there dreaming of freedom, blotting out the dingy reality of life back at home. He probably felt, as he idly watched the river traffic passing up and down and listened to the gentle lapping of the water, that this was the life, that the world was at his feet with golden opportunities just around the corner. Opportunities for fun; opportunities to make a little ready cash. All sorts of things were possible in Bangkok. So there he was in the breathless air, dreaming no doubt of adventure, when Charlie and Will appeared from inside the hotel.

He heard a cry of 'There you are, Dad!' and looked up to see two lank, terrifyingly skinny youths approaching him across the terrace. If it hadn't been for Charlie's height, he claimed later, he would hardly have recognized his own son, so thin had he grown and so brown.

Deirdre had been wrong to think that the boys wouldn't be too keen on seeing Harvey. They had been travelling on a shoestring and were by this time pretty short of funds. The opulence of the Oriental was certainly unlike anything they had come across in their wanderings and their hollow eyes lit up at the prospect of being offered dinner there. The tragedy of it was that on that first evening neither of them could eat very much. Who knows what germs lingered in their intestines?

Nothing delighted Harvey more, in somewhere like Bangkok, than the idea of making a deal, so having firmly convinced himself that a people as polite and smiling as the Thais must be predominantly honest, he was ready to trust almost any smiling villain who offered his services. And thus it was that on the following morning, while the boys were still asleep, he fell into the hands of one such charming and polite con man who picked him up outside his hotel.

Harvey's new friend, who introduced himself as Chuan, smiled and smiled, declaring himself as he did so to be an honest man. 'I like honest. You like honest. Me honest,' he announced. 'You like I show you Bangkok? Nice sights? Nice girls? You like little boys? I show you little boys. You like nice jewels?'

How could Harvey have been taken in?

When Will and Charlie eventually appeared from their cheap room on the other side of the city, they were amazed to find Harvey so excited, talking of sapphires and pearls and of someone called Chuan whom Harvey had invited to have a drink with him in the hotel. But Chuan had not wanted to come into the hotel; instead he had given Harvey a card with an address in another part of town where they were to meet later in the day.

During the few months that Will and Charlie had been travelling together, they had grown in wisdom and one of the first things that they had learned with a degree of sadness was not to trust people too easily. Certainly not to trust sleek, smiling men who made it their business to pick up Westerners outside their hotels with promises of deals. They both begged Harvey to forget all about Chuan and instead to go sightseeing with them.

Harvey was astounded by the boys' cynicism and rather cross with them. Where was their sense of adventure? Besides it annoyed him that they should presume to know so much more about Chuan than he did when they hadn't even met him. He, Harvey, had far more experience of the world than they had between them and furthermore he'd been in business one way or another almost all his life; if there was one thing he'd learned during all those years, it was how to sum people up. He could tell when a man was lying – he knew instinctively whether or not a man was a gentleman.

I don't know if, at that stage, either Will or Charlie knew anything about Harvey's dealings with Zed. If they did, they can hardly have been impressed by his professions of worldly wisdom.

In any case they all continued to argue for some time before it was finally decided that Harvey would go off on his own to see Chuan.

'And by the way, Dad, don't forget that tourists die like flies here,' Charlie apparently said with a trace of insolence in his voice. 'Be careful of anything you're offered.' He and Will then went off to seek their own adventures while Harvey hailed a taxi and handed the driver the card Chuan had given him with an address written on it.

It took some time to reach the destination and just as Harvey was standing on the pavement paying the taxi driver, Chuan suddenly appeared at his elbow, as if from nowhere, bowing and smiling obsequiously.

'You like honest, I like honest,' Chuan started his litany again. 'You like pretty little Thai girl? I make special price. Special girl . . .'

Momentarily Harvey must have wondered if the boys hadn't been talking a certain amount of sense, but then perhaps he told himself that Chuan was only behaving according to the mores of his culture. Very polite, very accommodating, wishing to be helpful. There could be no harm in that. And who knows, perhaps Harvey had taken advantage of such offers in the past.

'Sapphires, remember,' he said. 'I'd like to buy some sapphires.'

'Ah, yes, sir, sapphires. We go to see my brother-in-law.'

Chuan's brother-in-law was a most reputable jeweller who would of course make a special price for any friend of Chuan's and suddenly, it seemed, Harvey was a very good friend of Chuan's.

'Follow me,' Chuan commanded grandly and set off along the busy pavement winding his way in and out of the crowds at quite a pace.

Harvey must have looked conspicuous indeed as he strode behind Chuan, despite his long legs desperately trying to keep up, head and shoulders above everyone else, sweat pouring down his face, his shirt between his shoulderblades drenched. They seemed to walk for miles, Harvey forever bumping into people and bending to apologize. He claimed later that he had accidentally knocked a man's hat off with his arm swinging at his side.

They walked down wide pavements and crossed broad boulevards until finally they turned into a maze of smaller streets, where Harvey began to think he might get totally lost and where he wondered if he would ever be able to find a taxi. Chuan was still darting along ahead. Finally he stopped and waited for the breathless, sweating Harvey to catch up with him.

'This my brother's shop,' he said, leading the way through a darkened doorway and up a narrow flight of stairs.

'I thought he was your brother-in-law,' Harvey dared to say.

'Brother – brother-in-law, no problem,' said Chuan agreeably as he climbed on up.

Despite, he claims, the first genuine stirrings of suspicion, Harvey was feeling excited – young again, I suppose, and carefree.

As Harvey's is the only evidence we have for the whole of this episode it is, not surprisingly, difficult to discern exactly where truth merges into fiction, particularly with regard to what happened next. Did Chuan's brother/brother-in-law in fact have only one eye? Was there really a marmalade cat sitting in a jade basket, wearing pearl earrings? I rather doubt it. Did the jeweller run the sapphires through his fingers like handfuls of corn? Did he threaten Harvey with a stiletto, thus forcing him to part with his money? We don't know. But it is surely true that he boasted of the quality of his sapphires, of their size and depth of colour, as he held them up to the light and squinted at them through an eyeglass firmly clasped by brow and cheekbone to his one good eye.

And what we do know for sure is that Harvey spent a considerable amount of money – two or three thousand pounds perhaps – which he charged to his American Express card, on bags full of jewels like sweets. The jeweller claimed that he could send them duty free to England. No problem, of course. But at this point Harvey became suspicious. What if the jewels never turned up and he had already parted with his money? Harvey decided then that he would have to take them with him. He was confident that he would be able to stride through the customs without any trouble and that once he was back in London he would be able to sell the sapphires at an enormous profit, more than covering the cost of his trip to the East. He didn't regard what he planned to do as smuggling because, by some spurious twist of logic, he had decided that for smuggling to be smuggling, it had to be done repeatedly. A once-off thing hardly counted.

'No problem,' the jeweller said on hearing that Harvey planned to take the stones away there and then. 'I make nice package,' and so saying he apparently disappeared into a back room with the gems and returned a little while later with a carefully tied parcel.

Presumably as the result of a fleeting expression of mistrust which must have crossed Harvey's face when, smiling and bowing, the one-eyed jeweller handed over the ready-made packet, Chuan began to proclaim his brother's honesty.

'You are making very good business,' he said as he led the way back down to the street, where he soon found a taxi into which he bundled Harvey with instructions for him to be returned to the Oriental Hotel.

Later, by the time Will and Charlie met up with Harvey again, Harvey had already persuaded himself of the brilliance of the whole operation. There was no doubt in his mind that Chuan's friend – or brother – did it matter? – was a bona fide jeweller and a very decent man at that. Harvey was delighted with his purchases and somewhat disdainful of the boys who had spent the afternoon happily sightseeing. They had taken a boat upstream away from the concrete jungle of modern Bangkok to where the water hyacinths spread their shiny compact leaves across the surface of the river, where houses, from whose terraces smiling, cheerful children wave, rise on stilts from the water, where time appears to have no meaning.

Harvey was fed up with all that. He didn't want to talk about time having no meaning; he was only interested in the huge profit he was about to make from his sapphires. He could think of nothing else.

When a couple of days later Harvey was packing his bags to return home, he suddenly began to feel a little uneasy about being caught by the British customs as he came into the country with his booty. He was pretty sure that he would be able to walk through the 'Nothing to Declare' gate without any trouble, but what if they did stop him? Not only would he lose all his jewels but there would be a hefty fine as well. Harvey no doubt thought that at his age he might look a bit of a fool coming home from a few days in the East only to be caught at Heathrow with a sack of gemstones. At that point he must have decided to enlist the boys' help.

Will and Charlie were planning to spend a few days visiting the coast and the islands in the south before coming on back to England as their time was up and they had, in any case, run out of money. They were sitting, each with a backpack between his knees, having a final drink with Harvey on the terrace of the Oriental, when Harvey brought the subject up.

Will was immediately extremely embarrassed at the suggestion that it would be a good idea if he and Charlie brought the stones home, and angered at the implication that Harvey would make it worth their while. Will had no intention of helping but he wasn't quite sure how to refuse to do something for someone who had just been treating him to endless drinks and meals and taxis and who was the father of a friend. Charlie, however, had no such scruples.

'You must be crazy, Dad,' he said, 'if you think we're going to do your dirty work! Anyway,' he added sourly, 'what do you know about jewels? I bet that man's sold you a load of crap. They're probably all glass anyway.'

'Actually,' Will joined in rather more politely, 'I'm not sure it would be a very good idea because they do tend to search backpackers – especially men: and especially if they're coming from somewhere like Bangkok.'

'Oh, nonsense!' Harvey had the nerve to say. 'And it's not as if I was asking you to bring in a kilogramme of cocaine.'

Charlie was furious. 'We're not taking them, Dad. Geddit?' He put his two hands out palm-down in front of him and swept them apart. 'You can either chuck them away or declare them and pay the tax.'

After that Harvey sulked and they finished their drinks in an awkward silence before the boys decided that the time had come for them to be on their way.

'I must have a pee before we go,' Charlie said as he unwound his long body from his chair and disentangled his legs from his backpack.

'Good idea,' said Will and followed Charlie across the terrace into the hotel.

Harvey must have thought remarkably quickly and acted quickly as well, for by the time the two boys came back he had taken the packet of sapphires out of his pocket, unwrapped them and poured little handfuls of stones into a couple of pockets in each of the boys' backpacks. Loose like that he didn't think the customs would find them. He almost thought, I think, that the boys wouldn't find them either. If they did, they would have no alternative but to bring them home and hand them over. He stood up as they came back to the table and looked at his watch; he'd be leaving for the airport in half an hour. Charlie and Will shouldered their backpacks and fastened them round their hips, thanking Harvey as they did so for his hospitality. He shook them both warmly by the hand and they turned to go.

'See you in the Scrubs,' Charlie said with a bitter edge to his voice as he strode away.

Harvey laughed – a funny sort of laugh, Will thought later.

For the next few days neither Charlie nor Will considered unpacking. They stayed in a beach hut on the island of Ko Samui, lazing about and doing very little, I should imagine, and as for clothing, they pulled crumpled T-shirts out of their bags and crammed sweaty ones back in. They would soon – only too soon – be back in their mothers' nice clean houses with nice washing machines and nice baths and they weren't worried about comfort or, for that matter, much about cleanliness in those last days. In any case there was always the sea.

When they got back to the hostel in Bangkok where they

spent one night before catching the plane home, Will suddenly announced that his backpack stank, that it was almost impossible to shut it and that it was half full of dirty sandals and smelly T-shirts he thought he might as well throw away. He was going to repack the whole thing.

Charlie said he couldn't be bothered to do the same. It wasn't worth the effort, so he remained lying on his bed, his arms folded behind his head, watching as Will tipped the rather unsavoury contents of the body of the pack out on the floor. When he had sorted through his things and chucked a few to one side to the accompaniment of some coarse remarks from Charlie, he began to unzip the smaller side pockets, which was of course when he discovered the sapphires.

At first he couldn't think what they were. Little bits of blue glass? Pebbles from the beach?

'You idiot! Don't say you've been buying jewels too!' Charlie was amazed. 'And you never bloody let on.'

It took a few moments for Will to persuade his friend that he had no idea how these things had got into his pack and that he certainly hadn't bought them.

All of a sudden the truth dawned on Charlie and with a cry of 'The shit!' he leaped off his bed and began furiously to empty the contents of his pack all over the floor. Will couldn't think what had come over him until through a haze of unbelief the idea gradually presented itself that these indeed were Harvey's sapphires. But how the hell had they got into his bag? Charlie was meanwhile standing there beside him shaking his pack, unzipping it, throwing things about and swearing. It wasn't long before he too had found a handful of little blue stones.

The two of them soon worked out that the only time Harvey had been in any position to put the stones in their bags was when they had abandoned them briefly on the terrace of the hotel to go to the lavatory. They only wished they had discovered the jewels earlier.

'We could at least have flogged them,' Charlie said forlornly. As it was, they had to leave at crack of dawn for the airport.

Will consoled him with the idea that the sapphires were almost certainly made of glass, although neither boy had any way of telling. They tried biting them and cutting the glass of the window with them but the fact was that they had no idea what the results of their experiments ought to be.

During the months Will and Charlie had spent together abroad they had had one or two close shaves – a few hairy experiences. They both felt that they had extricated themselves well from some difficult situations. There were escapades they would never want anyone back home to know about, moments they were ashamed of and times when they had been downright lucky; now, at the eleventh hour, just as they were about to return to the comforts and comparative safety of home, they had no intention of chancing an arm by smuggling Harvey's sapphires into the country. For what if they really were sapphires?

They talked about what to do into the early hours and in the first light of morning they buckled on their packs and before catching the bus to the airport they walked down to the river and ceremoniously chucked Harvey's stones into the water.

A few days later Charlie rang Will from Somerset.

'Guess what Mum found in her washing machine?' he asked. 'The one that escaped. A bloody great sapphire among the T-shirts. And I'm not giving it to Dad.'

Charlie took that stone to a jeweller, who declared it to be a low-grade sapphire of little value, shallow, flawed and of a poor blue. Not worth very much at all.

'There are sapphires and sapphires, you see,' he had said.

Chapter XI

History doesn't relate what Penelope thought about Harvey's attempts to use his and her son to smuggle jewels back from the East, but it is easy to imagine that she cannot have been best pleased. Deirdre would have been very angry indeed about the whole affair, had her anger not been mitigated by the thought of Will and Charlie ceremoniously throwing the sapphires into the river at dawn.

'What on earth did you ever see in him?' Will, with the casual brutality of youth, asked his mother at one point.

'Oh, I don't know,' Deirdre had answered. Then, 'I think he was tall.' Or something like that.

On returning to this country neither boy could settle to anything; despite parental pressure they were both quite devoid of any idea as to what they might do next. They agreed that they didn't want to be in an office, that they didn't want to spend the rest of their lives being bossed around, that they never wanted to have to wear a suit or have a mortgage or get up in the morning at hours which they might find inconvenient. They didn't want to take any more exams, or to work from nine to five or to have to pay taxes.

Charlie rather thought he might like to join a band but he couldn't remember where he'd left the saxophone which had been bought for him at considerable expense a few years earlier and in which he had apparently lost interest remarkably soon. He might have left it in a friend's house, but that friend was in Canada. He couldn't ring his friend's mother because she was remarried and as Charlie couldn't remember her name he had no means of finding the telephone number.

'Just like Harvey,' Deirdre wanted to say, but it occurred to her that unfortunately Will, too, seemed at the time to be remarkably like Harvey.

Will was mooching moodily around the house, talking about making money in the most unlikely and unrealistic fashion. Having narrowly escaped being stopped for smuggling sapphires, he was thinking of going back to India and bringing home a few silver bangles with which to finance his trip. You could make a bomb on them, he was sure. You only had to get a stand in the Portobello Road. He didn't appear to have noticed that such bangles were already swamping the British market throughout the length and breadth of the land, but nevertheless he finally dropped the idea as much through inertia as anything else.

During all this time he remained good friends with Charlie and saw quite a lot of him. Charlie was living with his father in London and, having failed to find his saxophone, had eventually taken a job as a tennis coach in a private boys' school while Will, driven by boredom and poverty and much to his mother's amusement, at last found work as a hospital porter.

Harvey was clearly glad of Charlie's presence at home. His relationship with Moira seemed to have reached an all-time low; she, if Will was to be believed, brought endless streams of casual lovers back to the house, careless of Harvey's reaction. God knows how the small child fared. Will reported that he was alternately spoilt and neglected and that when Charlie wasn't working he spent a great deal of time looking after Frederick, carting him around with him like a mascot, feeding him on junk food since there was never anything to eat in the house and telling him exaggerated tales of his and Will's adventures in the East. Frederick became devoted to Charlie and the two made a rather engaging pair.

Naturally Harvey had soon grown bored with his role as cook and childminder. He was away from home a good deal of the time but no one really knew what he was up to. He certainly wasn't talking as much as usual about his affairs, which gave one to suppose that he might not be quite his usual optimistic self.

Then suddenly the talk was all of cricket again and every weekend Harvey was off somewhere – to Taunton to watch Somerset play Surrey, or to Old Trafford or to Headingly. He could think of nothing else and certainly where county cricket was concerned he always supported Somerset, taking a remarkably pompous line about the heady days when Botham and Viv Richards adorned the side. Since they had gone, discipline in Somerset was much tighter and this, according to Harvey, was an excellent thing.

Sometimes Charlie and Frederick went off to watch the cricket with Harvey, Charlie and Harvey both swearing that Frederick was born to be a star. At the tender age of five he apparently already displayed precocious athleticism and had a remarkable eye for a ball. When Will was not working at weekends, he very often went too. They stayed in bed-and-breakfasts up and down the country with Harvey as often as not footing the bill, or sometimes they stayed with old, half-forgotten – suddenly conveniently remembered – friends of

Harvey's who happened to have nice, comfortable country houses in the neighbourhood of whichever county ground they were planning to attend.

The accident happened one weekend when all four of them had gone to Taunton to watch Somerset play Worcestershire. Will, who had recently been going out with a student nurse from the hospital where he worked, had been hoping to spend the weekend with her and had not meant to go to watch the cricket, but to his chagrin his nurse suddenly announced that she would be working for most of the weekend and that on Sunday evening, which she had off, she planned to go and see her mother.

Deirdre was at first delighted by the appearance on the scene of the student nurse, but as she began to blow hot and cold, Deirdre became exasperated. Will grew moody again. So, although Deirdre felt uncomfortable about the amount of time Will spent with Harvey, she was on this occasion somewhat relieved when he said that he would be away in Taunton with the Hothams for the weekend. She had a few days off and didn't relish the idea of having Will slouching around the house in a bad temper, picking quarrels, forever taking the high moral tone common to so many of the younger generation.

On the Saturday morning the four of them set out first thing in Harvey's car. Charlie's promised car had somehow never materialized and consequently Charlie hadn't got round to passing his test. Will had failed his twice and for some time had lost any incentive to try again since he couldn't imagine ever having a car in the foreseeable future and anyway he didn't really need one in London. Deirdre, who had an almost neurotic horror of young men driving, accelerating dangerously to affirm their manhood, was quite relieved about that, and not so pleased when Will suddenly changed his mind and, with what his mother regarded as a remarkable stroke of luck, managed to pass at the third attempt.

They were expected back on Sunday night.

But at nine o'clock on Sunday evening the telephone rang and Deirdre, to her surprise when she answered it, heard Harvey's voice. Immediately a pang of fear gripped her.

'Where are you?' she said. 'What's happened?'

The news was very bad. Harvey was ringing from the hospital in Taunton. There had been an accident. Could Deirdre come as soon as possible? This on a Sunday evening meant getting into a car and driving. At that time of night it ought not to take much more than about two and a half hours.

Will was unconscious and was being seen by the doctor at the moment. No one could tell yet quite how serious it was. No one else was hurt; at least that's what Harvey said at the time. Perhaps he didn't quite dare tell Deirdre the worst over the telephone.

In fact it later turned out that a child had been killed.

Harvey was pretty fed up by the end of the day. After watching the match in brilliant sunshine with cricket being just like cricket ought to be – all green and white and graceful – he was thoroughly disgusted that Somerset was beaten. Mind you, he grumbled, he could see it coming as they hadn't been doing at all well lately. He was almost tempted to wish for a return to the good old days of Richards and Botham. He decided he needed a drink before hitting the road; they might stop in a nice pub he knew for some supper.

At this point Charlie made up his mind to ring his mother, to see if he could stay the night at home as he didn't have to be back in London until the following afternoon and could catch a bus up in the morning. Penelope was delighted at the prospect of seeing her son and gladly agreed to pick him up in Taunton, which left Will and Frederick to travel back with Harvey.

Harvey was full of opinions as to how Somerset could improve their game and quite a rowdy conversation took place in the garden of the pub where he stopped for supper with Will and Frederick. People remembered afterwards that Harvey had caused quite a stir and several locals had joined in. There was the pro-Botham faction and the anti faction. There were those who remembered a certain innings from the mid-eighties or a particular over, there were others who bathed in the reflected glory of having bumped into Viv Richards in the bank or Joel Garner at the railway station. Little Frederick sat quietly beside his father, engrossed in a plate of chips, eyelids dropping from exhaustion. Will didn't say very much.

It is easy to picture Harvey there at that pub in the Quantocks, out in the garden on a summer's evening, holding forth, legs stretched in front of him, waving his arms, demonstrating how to bowl, showing off, knowing best, the Londoner in the midst of country bumpkins, yet the old Somerset hand. Harvey would have been in his element, ordering drinks all round, downing a pint or two of beer and then two or three double whiskies, making everyone laugh, the heart and soul of the party, dropping the names of local villages, possibly talking about his old village team, heedless of Frederick's tender years and exhaustion, oblivious to Will. He may even have made a few ill-timed jokes about one for the road.

Harvey always was someone who believed himself to be above any generally inconvenient laws or by-laws. He certainly considered himself to bear a charmed life where the drinking and driving laws were concerned. For one thing, being a big man, he supposed that he could drink far more than average without it showing up on the breathalyser. He also firmly believed – or at least paid lip-service to the belief – that he drove better with a little bit of alcohol inside him than he did stone cold sober. In any case it never occurred to him that he was ever likely to be stopped and submitted by some pert young policeman to the indignities of a test. He knew his capacity; he knew the limits beyond which he ought not to drive; he'd been driving for thirty-something years without any problem and so forth . . . blah . . . blah . . . blah . . .

Despite all this, Harvey told Deirdre that that evening, as they left the pub, he suddenly felt nervous about the long drive home and about the amount he had drunk. Will hadn't had much, so he thought that the wisest thing to do would be to let Will drive. Never mind that Will had only recently passed his test and had had very little experience of driving outside London. He certainly wasn't used to country lanes or motorways.

So Frederick was put in the back where he immediately fell asleep, Will drove and Harvey sat beside Will in the passenger seat. It's easy to envisage him, still talking no doubt, probably even waving his arms in front of Will's eyes, going on about silly mid-off and forward short leg and about how he had always dreamed of playing for Surrey, but how it was, alas, too late now.

The car wound erratically up over the hills – Harvey claimed later that he was a bit nervous, since Will, he said, drove alternately with frightening panache and girlish hesitation. The road there is far from straight and that day, at that hour, the lengthening rays of the evening sun cast long shadows, whilst the breathtaking view down across gently undulating farmland to where the River Parrett meanders through the Levels out to Bridgwater Bay might be enough at the best of times to distract the attention of even the most seasoned driver.

Harvey's car was a big, heavy Rover over which Will appeared to have only minimum control as he swung it uneasily round bends and accelerated unnervingly into whatever little straight there was. As they went uphill, slightly too fast into a blind corner, Harvey remembered admonishing Will to be careful; then, just as they hurtled round the corner, they saw the boy on the bicycle, there in the middle of the lane.

And then it happened – in horrible slow motion. The car hit the bicycle and the boy – a boy of about ten with ginger hair – flew into the air so gracefully spreadeagled in the fading light and landed with a thump on the bonnet of the car, off which he slowly bounced before turning over and over, it seemed, flailing with his arms almost like a spent swimmer struggling for breath and crashing on his face by the side of the road.

The car swerved horribly, Will, as Harvey explained, having completely lost control, and crashed headlong into a tree growing out of the hedge. Will, who was not wearing his seat belt, was thrown forward and knocked unconscious; Frederick began to howl as he was jolted to the floor between the back seat and the driver's seat, but, in the event, he, like Harvey, escaped with bruises.

The first thing Harvey did was to leap from the car – mercifully he could open the door – and run to the child in the road who lay there apparently lifeless. Not a car had passed and it was some way back to the last house. Harvey didn't feel he could leave the scene although he desperately needed help. He glanced at the car with Will, still unconscious, slumped over the wheel and was suddenly terrified that it might burst into flames. He knew that it could be dangerous to move Will but he couldn't risk leaving him trapped in the car, so, having got Frederick out, he managed with some difficulty to lift Will out too, and to lay him on the grass by the edge of the road.

Luckily it was only a few minutes later that a couple of cars came by in quick succession, both of which stopped. The driver of the first car hurried immediately on to ring for an ambulance. At this point it seemed that the child in the road must be dead but a girl travelling in the second car with her boyfriend was determined to give him the kiss of life, which she did to no avail. There was no life in him. He lay there, still, in grubby jeans, trainers and a sky-blue T-shirt; an archetypal boy with a freckled face. His mangled bike lay in a disconsolate heap a few yards down the lane.

It seemed an age, Harvey said, before the police and ambulance arrived but the young couple from the second car waited with him, the girl mostly consoling Frederick, who was crying. She took him by the hand and led him along the grass bank away from the accident, talking to him gently. Harvey and the young man were left not knowing quite what to do, with Will unconscious but breathing on the verge and the red-headed boy whom they daren't touch lying in the road. It having been a warm summer's day, there were no coats or rugs in the car with which to cover the wounded. They moved the bicycle out of the way and put a red breakdown triangle from the boot of Harvey's car in the lane. Two or three cars went by before the ambulance arrived. These Harvey waved on, saying that help was on the way but begging them to ring for an ambulance all the same, just to make double sure. One car stopped and disgorged three middle-aged women all eager to take control, but at just that moment an ambulance arrived with a police car howling in hot pursuit.

On her way down to Taunton that night Deirdre had plenty of time to think and plenty of time to be afraid for the life of her only child. To begin with she felt very angry. Angry with Harvey for letting Will drive and angry too with Will for agreeing to drive, knowing, as perhaps he did, that he might be over the permitted alcohol limit. But most of her anger was directed at Harvey, unjustly perhaps, since it must be said that if Will was sober, perhaps it was more sensible that he should drive than that a drunken Harvey should. But Harvey, who had brought Deirdre nothing but unhappiness, had been banished from her life long ago and if it hadn't been for Will's chance friendship with Charlie, he would never, she felt sure, have re-emerged from the woodwork. Anyway, what was so special about Charlie? Except that, like Will, he hadn't done very well in his exams. Whichever way she turned, Deirdre felt engulfed by impotent rage. And what was the point of such anger when her son was lying senseless in hospital – for all she knew at death's door?

By the time Deirdre eventually reached the hospital Will had been X-rayed and had been seen by a doctor; he had also begun to show some signs of consciousness. The doctor was of the opinion that this was a bad case of concussion since there were no broken bones and there was no internal bleeding. All that could be done for the moment was to keep a close eye on the patient. The police were, of course, waiting eagerly in the wings to question him.

Deirdre was told that the little boy, called Jason, had been dead on arrival at hospital. There had been some difficulty in identifying him but his parents had now been informed. Deirdre felt sick and ashamed and mad. There was a dead child, killed by her son, and there was her son, probably going to live after all, and her only care was that Will should live and that somehow for his own sake, he should not have killed that boy. For that little dead child and his parents she felt nothing. She wished he had never existed, then she fancied that he might have bicycled in front of that car in some puerile suicide bid, to escape perhaps from a violent or abusive stepfather. Who could guess? Then she felt ashamed and appalled at her thoughts and turned them back to her own son by whose bed she sat, whose hand she held. 'Let him live,' she prayed to a god in whom she did not believe.

Harvey meanwhile had been questioned by the police and to his indignation breathalysed. The breathalyser had shown him to be substantially over the limit but that didn't really worry him since he had not been driving. His car was clearly unroadworthy and even if it had not been, the police would hardly have allowed him, in his condition, to set out for London. A burly policeman chucked little Frederick under the chin and attempted to ask him a few questions as he sat on the lap of a young WPC, but the child was stunned into silence and so it was thought best to release Harvey with his son. They went off in search of a bed and breakfast, having been asked to report to the police station in the morning before making any arrangements to return to London.

By the following morning Will had regained consciousness but could remember nothing of the accident although, for some reason, he was sure that he hadn't been driving. The last thing he remembered was getting into the car outside the pub. He remembered Harvey putting Frederick in the back and telling him to lie down and go to sleep. He remembered thinking what bad luck it was being a child and how unpleasant it would be for Frederick when he got back to London to have to be woken up, undressed and put to bed.

He even felt a bit guilty – altough it was hardly his responsibility – that they hadn't set out earlier.

The doctors of course wanted to keep the police from exciting Will too much. They would only allow them a few minutes at a time. Two policemen waited quietly in the corridor for permission to return to the patient's bedside.

When at last they were allowed back for a second inquisition, Will was as adamant as ever that he had not been driving. He remembered, he was certain, Harvey climbing into the driving seat. He even remembered not doing up his seat belt because he said he was feeling a bit sick, which was why he had drunk only one pint in the pub. He remembered Harvey driving up a certain hill, saying laughingly something about there not being many police cars on those lanes. Beyond that he could remember nothing.

Of course the essential witness was Frederick, who, bewildered and afraid and perhaps instinctively loyal to his father, refused to say anything despite the cajoling of the craftiest and most intuitive policemen and policewomen in the force, who talked sweetly and gave him coloured pencils and paper in the hopes that he would draw a picture of what had happened. Still he remained mute and merely scribbled over the paper in cheerful greens and blues, perhaps because, as Harvey was happy to point out, Frederick had been asleep when the accident happened.

No one but Harvey could surely ever presume the police to be so easily bamboozled. They can tell from a thousand things – not least the angle at which a person is bruised – exactly where that person was sitting in a car at the moment of collision. Then, as far as this accident was concerned, there was the evidence of people who had been in the pub that evening. At least two of them, wandering out at the time Harvey left, actually witnessed him getting into the driving seat. He could have claimed that he changed places with Will later, but the accident took place only about two miles from the pub; besides, Harvey had always claimed that Will was driving from the outset.

By early on Monday afternoon Harvey had been arrested and charged with driving while twice over the limit, with driving without due care and attention, with unlawfully killing Jason Chedzoy and with attempting to pervert the course of justice.

By the same time on Monday afternoon, it had become apparent that Will was not seriously hurt and that with a little rest he would soon make a full recovery; thus Deirdre found it in her heart to feel for Jason's parents.

The appalling awareness of just how far Harvey was prepared to go in his lies was a shock to us all.

Later I wondered at what point Deirdre first thought Harvey might be lying, but she told me that she never really suspected it until the police actually charged him. I found that hard to credit, but she had felt that Will's memory might well be faulty; after all, he had been unconscious for several hours and certainly had no memory of the accident itself. In any case she had been in such a state of shock that she had blindly believed what she was told, for who could imagine that even Harvey could drag an innocent, unconscious person from a car in an attempt to incriminate him? At any rate she was used to believing what people said. By the time Harvey was charged, all she felt was enormous relief. Relief for Will that he was all right and that he did not have to go through life with the death of a child on his conscience. For Harvey she felt nothing but disgust.

Back in London *Schadenfreude* reared its ugly head. Everyone who knew Harvey also knew some horror story about prison, about how someone like Harvey would have to be kept apart from the other prisoners, with paedophiles and sex offenders, for his own safety, otherwise he would be attacked. Anyway who could picture Harvey in prison? Harvey, of all people! How he would hate it!

Of course it wasn't certain that Harvey would be sent down. He had hired the most expensive lawyer he could find to argue his case, to whom he no doubt lied about the speed at which he had been travelling – forgetting that the police would have measured the skid marks – and for whom he would have invented some rigmarole whereby he hoped to lay the blame on the dead child. Harvey had a clean licence, which was one thing to his advantage, but his particular attempt to pervert the course of justice was hardly likely to find favour with a judge. People said with long faces, nodding their heads sagely, that he would probably get four years. 'Of course,' they added piously, 'it could happen to any one of us at any given time – just a moment's inattention and there you are . . .' They could all imagine killing a child, but no one could imagine doing what Harvey had done next.

Deirdre just longed for the whole thing to be over so that she could put it behind her and, more particularly, so that Will could. Will would naturally be called as a witness, which would be quite traumatic for him, and Deirdre felt that he would need her support, so she planned to attend the trial with him.

Harvey in the dock was sober-suited and penitent looking. He wore a black tie in deference to the dead child. Outside the court Mr and Mrs Chedzoy were filmed by West Country television baying for blood. They weren't going to get their Jason back and they thought Harvey should be hanged. For a moment Deirdre understood their uncontrolled rage. She remembered thinking that Will, too, was going to die.

Will gave his evidence quietly and with dignity, then the

passers-by who had stopped to help were called and a couple who had been in the pub earlier in the evening. With that and evidence from one of the ambulance crew who had attended the scene and from two police officers, the prosecution needed to say no more.

Harvey, who had pleaded not guilty to driving without due care and attention, had little that could be said in his defence, but his expensive London lawyer made a flowery speech stressing what a splendid man Harvey was, how he had driven for thirty-something years without so much as a blemish on his licence. He spoke of the child, Jason, wantonly darting across the road without so much as looking, he spoke of Harvey's remorse, of how he would carry the guilt of Jason's death for the rest of his life, and of how his attempt to lay the blame of what had happened on Will had been the act of a man in a state of shock, something quite out of character for Harvey and something which he had almost instantly retracted. He begged for leniency.

The judge was not a lenient judge. He took an extremely poor view of the whole affair. A man of Harvey's education and of Harvey's standing in society should set an example to others, not drive carelessly around country lanes in an intoxicated condition, heedless of the lives of innocent children. The judge found Harvey's behaviour to be callous and despicable. 'You are a cowardly man of little moral fibre,' he said, glowering at Harvey over his half-moon spectacles, 'and I sentence you to six years' imprisonment.'

Deirdre remembers burying her face in her hands at that moment. Poor old Harvey, she thought. Poor old Harvey!

Harvey was taken away and sent to an open prison somewhere and a lot of people felt sorry for him. Even Penelope apparently visited him in prison and, much against his mother's advice, so did Will, but one person who was unremitting in her contempt was Moira. No sooner had Harvey gone to prison than she instituted divorce proceedings. She complained that he was a drunk and a murderer, unfit to be the father of her little boy. And God alone knows how that poor little boy fared back at the hands of his mother. Charlie, I believe, continued as a good friend to him, but then Charlie wasn't there very often and as Will no longer saw Charlie, Deirdre no longer heard about what was happening.

With his usual *sang-froid* Harvey did his very best to turn prison to his own advantage – if such a thing is possible. To those who visited him he told endless tales of daring and devilry picked up from the old lags; he described his fellow inmates, told of friendships he had formed with them, boasted of the book he would write when he got out, claimed that the whole thing was preposterous in any case. That child had caused his own death. Then, at other times, he seemed to forget what had gone before and would return to his original story that Will had been driving. He, Harvey, was innocent. There had been a gross miscarriage of justice and he was waiting for an appeal to be heard.

Who knows what he felt alone at night? Is Harvey capable of feeling anything when he is alone at night? Did he review his life with anything approaching honesty? Did he feel isolated? Afraid? He must have wondered what he would do when he eventually came out. I am prepared to believe that he genuinely worried about what might happen to Frederick, although he admitted to several people that he was glad to be shot of Moira. Harvey read a lot in prison, which was perhaps something he hadn't done much of before, and he never whinged. Any complaint he had was generally expressed, brazenly, in the form of a joke.

Harvey was capable of bluffing his way through a lengthy

prison sentence. In the long run there was nothing that the oldest of old lags could teach Harvey.

He served three and a half years in the end and even while he was away in prison he was not forgotten. Every now and then his name would come up in conversation and somebody would surely have something to say about him. The *Schadenfreude* which had originally greeted his downfall had somehow been overtaken by a weird kind of hero-worship. The stories which circulated at this time were always about how Harvey had taken it like a man, about what rotten luck it was really – could have been any one of us – about his good humour, his nerve, his decency in fact. All sorts of people went to see him. People who had never been close friends, people who went, I suspect, to gain some extraordinary imagined kudos from visiting him, or some kind of reflected glory. Away in prison Harvey became enormously popular with many of those who remained outside. He had acquired glamour.

One wondered if the glamour would last, thus helping to see him through the difficult days that must lie ahead after his release. Who knew what would happen then? He would certainly need friends. Moira had divorced him and she remained in the London house with Frederick and – so people said – an increasingly undesirable assortment of casual lovers. Where would Harvey go? Who would welcome him back? Charlie, it appears, was living abroad and Catherine had long since decided that she didn't want to have anything to do with her father. She was even furious with her mother for taking pity on Harvey and visiting him in prison. He would certainly need those admiring friends when the time came.

As for Deirdre, she refused to waste her time thinking about Harvey. She had her work to do and with only a few years left before retirement she was busier than ever. Harvey had done his best in the early years to wreck her life and then later to wreck Will's. She had no wish for any further involvement of any kind and was glad that Will no longer saw Charlie and that Charlie was abroad out of temptation's way. She was much relieved, too, that Will had eventually decided to go back into higher education and was taking a degree in physics and engineering at Bristol University. Everything for the moment was going along all right. She didn't need to tempt fate. I think she probably felt that with Harvey away in prison, that was the end of Harvey's story. Perhaps I felt that, too.

Chapter XII

Over the years I have not infrequently wondered what it is about Harvey and my relationship with him that has caused me to allow myself to become so fascinated by him. Or is fascination really the right word? Sometimes I think I am obsessed with him or jealous of him. Perhaps I always have been jealous. At others I believe that I am motivated by a spirit of revenge – not that revenge is a pretty thing.

If I am to be honest with myself, I will have to go back to the very beginning, right back to the time when I first set eyes on him. I remember it clearly.

I do not think that I had ever been away from home alone until the terrible day dawned when, at the age of eight, I was left, a puny, miserable creature, to cry my eyes out in the dormitory of an averagely unpleasant boys' prep school. I had dreaded going despite the stories of future fun and high jinks with which my parents regaled me to encourage some kind of enthusiasm on my part. My father assured me that boarding school was the best fun in the world, and my mother, rather more hesitantly, tried to convince me that I would love it. When I left home that first time, my sisters in turn clasped me to them with tears rolling down their several cheeks and begged my parents to let me stay with them. As I was bundled into the back of our dark-green Wolseley, stunned with apprehension, I felt like a lamb being taken to the sacrifice. Perhaps that is what I was. In any case, just like hundreds of boys before me and hundreds more after me, I went, was homesick and hated it – at least for the first two years.

Of course I feared the unknown, but like most children, I feared more than anything else being different and, unfortunately, I was a little different. For one thing I was very small for my age, which usually resulted in my being given harmless nicknames like Squit or Titch, which I bore with equanimity. But in truth I just hated being small and longed to grow. Neither could I understand why I should be so small as both my parents were reasonably tall. My father, to whom I looked up with longing, was a good six foot. I imagined that one day I would surely reach his august height and when in church the clergyman announced a moment's silence for our own private prayers, I would beseech the Lord to make me tall. At some stage, I hasten to add, He must have listened since, by the time I reached man's estate, although smaller than my father, I was a reasonable size.

In addition to being small, I had, as the result of a difficult birth, a slightly twisted hip which has always made me walk with a limp. This limp, funnily enough, is not anything which has ever greatly bothered me. Of course I would have preferred not to have it but I do remember at a very early age learning to cope with it, to accept it and to accept the occasional discomfort it caused me. What I hated about it was not so much the inconvenience – the fact that I couldn't manage physically as well as other children and that I tired more easily – but the horror of being pointed at or laughed at because of it, and the horror of seeing other children whispering behind their hands about it, then looking quickly away. But worst of all I hated the concerned attention of caring grown-ups as they bent over me to enquire in sentimental voices if I could manage a flight of steps or needed a hand. Sometimes they would make some comment to each other – up there, over my head as if I couldn't hear or didn't exist outside their own sensitivities. They'd say things like, 'Poor little mite, it's so unfair,' leaving me – poor little mite indeed – to cringe at their gracelessness and to wish myself dead.

All of this made going away to boarding school especially difficult since I knew what was inevitably in store for me and I dreaded having to go through with it.

I don't in fact, thank God, remember very much about the first few days or weeks at that school. I remember feeling lonely and crying a lot and having no friends and I remember the crowding and the lack of privacy and the smell of the corridors, but I don't remember many incidents in detail. I suppose I kept my head down, kept myself to myself and probably read a good deal. Biggles, I suppose, and *Stalky & Co.* I think I read a number of things in those days which I didn't understand. I was quite good at my books so I imagine that I concentrated on my work as a consolation for not being able to play games and for having no friends. Although at night I occasionally heard snuffles from one or two of the beds in the dormitory, the other boys all appeared to me to be so confident, tall, handsome and boisterous.

But there was one boy who more than any other captured my attention. He was very tall for his age so that I had at first imagined him to be a couple of years older than myself, he was dark and lackadaisical with a humorous, languid look and he always seemed to be talking and making the other boys laugh. I noticed him on that very first evening of term standing there in the middle of what was known as the junior boys' common room. There was a slightly subdued, beginning-of-term atmosphere about the place. One or two of the older boys were pushing and shoving each other in corners; someone had some conkers. A fat boy with spectacles and big red knees sticking out under his grey flannel shorts was making a noise like an ack-ack gun as he aimed an imaginary weapon slowly round the room, and there was Harvey – a new boy like myself, as I was later to discover – the only one to have reached the required height to be allowed to wear long trousers, looking quite at home, knees bent, hands clenched round an invisible bat. Suddenly, with a graceful movement he took a step forward with his left leg and thrust his hands out and up with a loud cry of 'Howzat!'

At that instant I certainly envied Harvey. I envied his confidence and style and perhaps a seed of hero-worship was sown.

For about a year I did nothing but admire Harvey from afar, as it never entered my head that this tall, athletic boy could ever become my friend and neither do I suppose that he noticed me very much during that time. Other boys teased me, just as I had feared they would, making my life a misery, but as I soon came to realize, they had begun to mock Harvey too. He had come to be regarded as a bumptious boy, much too pleased with himself, in need of squashing. Having initially made himself quite popular with his wit and prowess at games, Harvey was suddenly as unloved as I was. I, as I say, still admired him from a distance, but guessing at his loneliness, I had started to feel sorry for him too, and he, wandering lonesome about the school, was in no position to revile my hesitant overtures.

Thus our friendship was born.

I came then to love Harvey with a fierce love, not just because I was grateful for his friendship which flattered me, but because I delighted in his company. He made me laugh and he liked me, so we became inseparable and between us formed a front which brought us not only self-respect but the respect of our peers as well. With a friend like Harvey, life at school was transformed.

Despite his complete lack of moral fibre, I think that there was always something about Harvey which I wanted but could not have, something which if I could admire it in him as a friend, I might feel I had myself gained vicariously. Harvey's height gave me stature. Harvey's athleticism gave me kudos. I might be small and lame and pale, but my friend was tall and handsome and, as I saw it, virile.

Things went well until the first terrible betrayal.

The cool disdain of Harvey's parents when he took me to stay in Scotland hurt me a little but I shrugged it off, dazzled by what I saw as the glamour of Harvey's home compared to mine. His parents, who were old, or so I thought, seemed so sophisticated and grand after mine that I hardly expected to be noticed by them. The fact that his mother so obviously admired Harvey and appeared to defer to him all the time only increased my sense of admiration for my friend. But Harvey at home did not treat me quite as he did at school. In front of his parents at least, he became cold and supercilious, which was something that at the time I simply couldn't understand, although I do remember feeling hurt by it.

Things were different when Harvey came to stay at home with me. For one thing my mother treated him as a hero. My mother was a warm-hearted, natural woman who loved her children and therefore welcomed any friend of theirs with the kindness that was her hallmark. I also believe that she was glad to think that at last I had made a friend and was happier at school. My four older sisters all treated Harvey as a huge, likeable joke, which delighted him. He delighted too, I think, in the happy-go-lucky family atmosphere of my home, so unlike the starched coldness of his own. He was nice to me again and everything seemed all right until we went back to school.

Childish though it may seem, I sometimes wonder if I have ever yet really forgiven Harvey for all the lies he invented about himself and one after another of my sisters. My oldest sister, Angela – the one who is friends with Penelope – laughed about it when she was told years later and just said, 'Typical Harvey.' Sometimes even now she annoys me by referring to what at the time I regarded as a vile betrayal and laughs again in an irritating fashion.

That first great betrayal certainly made me wary of Harvey so that I never again trusted him in quite the same way as I had done before. I looked at him differently and watched how he treated other people. But I still loved him. He still had something that I needed. And I apparently still had something that he needed – until we moved on to our next school.

At public school, it may be remembered, Harvey, finding himself to be a glamorous attraction – sporting star – in a new land of opportunity, turned his back entirely on me, denying our earlier friendship.

It may seem strange that I didn't wash my hands of him there and then; he had washed his of me. In fact we just avoided each other for a few years and I made other friends, grew up, at last grew taller, worked hard, did well at school without ever falling into the trap of becoming a swot and, despite a terrible, lingering fascination with Harvey, managed not to allow him to bother me. But I know that somewhere inside me I still longed to be more like him. He boasted of his experiences with girls and I, believing or at least half believing everything he said, longed for his much-vaunted *savoir faire*.

By the time we were in the sixth form, things between us had settled down and we superficially became friends again.

Because of my hip, I was exempt from national service and so while I was at Oxford and Harvey was away, among other things making a nuisance of himself in Cyprus, our paths diverged so that we didn't see each other for some time. We met up again later in London and now that we were grown-up, our childhood quarrels seemed to be buried – Harvey was just an old friend. Someone I had always known. I saw him surrounded by bright and beautiful people and, if I am honest, I suppose my latent admiration for him and my secret longing to be more like him reasserted itself. I happily attached myself to his circle.

I cannot truthfully say when it was that I first fell in love with Deirdre. Sometimes I feel as if I have always loved her. All those years ago when she was Harvey's shy, unfathomable bride, there were those who thought of her as dreary and uninteresting, unworthy of Harvey's panache. During those weekends we spent at Shackles with her so withdrawn, so quietly uncommunicative, I used to watch her and wonder what she thought. I always felt that there were hidden depths to Deirdre and my heart ached for her when I saw how badly Harvey treated her. But it did not occur to me in those days that I loved her; only that I liked her very much indeed, that I always felt comfortable with her and that I always looked forward to seeing her. I do remember thinking that she was far prettier and probably far more intelligent than she realized. Certainly more intelligent than Harvey, I used to think. I wondered how it would all turn out, but she was Harvey's wife and Harvey, despite everything, was my friend so it never entered my head to think of her in any other terms. Perhaps I should have taken my revenge on Harvey then. How different my life would have been!

But who can say? Now that I am married to Deirdre, I am as happy as I have ever been. There is no point in weeping over the years we spent apart.

When I came back from abroad after the break-up of my first marriage and, out of the blue, Deirdre rang me that evening, my heart leaped up, not because my intentions were anything but innocent since I knew of her remarriage, but just because she was Deirdre and I still loved her.

I had often thought of her during an unhappy, childless marriage and during all those years in the East. She was the fantasy perfect partner to whom my mind always returned in my darkest hours. Not anyone's perfect partner – just mine.

When I was told of Deirdre's marriage to Ralph I felt acutely jealous, but paradoxically I also remember feeling elated and happy for Deirdre. I was in no position to marry her and I very sincerely wanted her to be happy. I wanted her to be happy and I wanted Harvey to realize what he had lost, because in those faraway places I thought almost as much about Harvey as I did about Deirdre. I could never quite get him out of my system and often wondered what he was up to.

I wondered if he was still flitting through life, apparently without a care in the world, taking everyone – most of all himself – for a ride. At some point I even thought of writing a novel with Harvey as the main character; indeed I thought long and hard about it, but I was too busy then, so the whole thing never materialized.

About a year after my return to London Ralph had a massive stroke. He was rushed to hospital, where for two or three days he hovered between life and death before suffering a second, this time fatal, stroke. Though their marriage had not been founded on passion, Deirdre was undoubtedly fond of Ralph and they had been happy together. But Ralph was so much older than Deirdre that somewhere in her mind she had prepared herself for an early, prolonged widowhood, which, although it may have helped her ultimately to cope with her bereavement, did not mitigate the shock of sudden death. Once again I was around with a shoulder for Deirdre to cry on.

Eighteen months later, just before Will and Charlie came back from India, we were married.

It was a strange feeling after so many years of leading our separate lives, to find the three of us – Harvey, Deirdre and myself – together again, but differently realigned. This time Harvey was the outsider and in a funny way I sensed that he was now jealous of me. There were the two people for whom he had been once some kind of a hero, united at last and both of them in better shape than he was. Yet we both felt haunted by Harvey. We felt sorry for him and angry with him by turns, and Deirdre in particular just wished she could forget him, as indeed she had more or less succeeded in doing until Will brought him back into her life via Charlie.

Harvey, it appeared, was delighted to be in contact with Deirdre again so that he seemed to be always hanging around, wanting some sort of approval or, like a small child, just wanting to be noticed. No doubt under his ebullient exterior he was unhappy and the combined force of Deirdre and myself may have presented itself as something he could cling to. I think he encouraged Charlie's friendship with Will and even tried to become part of it as a path back to Deirdre whose attitude towards him he may have imagined to have been softened by me.

At the time I am speaking of, Harvey's private life was a

complete shambles, he was financially falling on hard times with no apparent means of improving his situation. Perhaps he feared to be alone in case he had to confront the truth, the truth of course being something which Harvey has assiduously ever avoided.

I remember him coming round for a drink one evening just after the boys had gone abroad. Deirdre was still at the hospital and as we sat in the sitting room with our drinks, Harvey began to tell me about his life, as if I didn't know enough about it already. He began by telling me a totally invented version of the break-up of his marriage to Deirdre, forgetting, I suppose, that I had been very much around at the time and obviously wanting to draw a veil over quite how badly he had behaved then. Anyone who had not met him before might well have been conned into thinking that it was he who had been badly treated and that he had emerged from the whole thing a hero.

Suddenly I felt rather cross. I wished Harvey would go away – certainly before Deirdre came back. 'Don't you remember Frances and poor old, long-suffering George?' I asked a little harshly.

Harvey instantly changed gear. He was off and away. Frances was quite the most beautiful woman he had ever seen in his life but as cold as ice. George was of no account. Harvey couldn't think why Frances had ever married him in the first place.

'By all accounts they're still together,' I said.

Harvey then invented some lie – well, if it was true it was so by sheer coincidence – about Frances having been the lover of some cabinet minister for years. It was obvious to me that he just didn't want George to be the winner.

Then Harvey started on George. He told some convoluted story of crooked deals and chicanery in which George was supposed to be involved and of how George was paying blackmail to keep the story out of the press. Harvey, stuttering slightly now, absolutely swore that this was true.

So Harvey hadn't changed then and Harvey, I am sure, never will change. If ever a man was swallowed into the vortex of his own lies, that man is Harvey.

On the evening of the accident, I drove Deirdre down to Taunton; when we reached the hospital, Harvey was there to welcome us, telling us of the indignities he had suffered at the hands of the police. Deirdre hardly listened – she was concerned only for Will. There was a policeman at the hospital who, as soon as Deirdre had been led away by a nurse to her son's bedside, took me aside and told me the bad news about the child having been killed. I didn't know how we were going to break it to Deirdre and then I looked at Harvey and Harvey was looking at the floor and he, I was certain, was thinking up some lies. At that moment I hated him. Hadn't he caused us all enough trouble over the years? I had a gut feeling that the whole truth about this accident had not yet been told but I was confused and couldn't imagine exactly where the deception lay. I was simply aware that Harvey was not telling the truth. I had known him long enough.

Deirdre and I spent the whole of that night in the hospital, she at the patient's bedside and I mostly pacing the corridor. By morning Will was making rapid progress and then, at about three o'clock in the afternoon, we heard that Harvey had been arrested and charged. All morning the police had been hovering around outside the ward, snatching every permitted ten minutes in which to ask questions.

Harvey, who was to appear in court the following morning, then had the nerve to come and find me. 'I say, old boy . . .' I was pleased to see that he was looking a bit hangdog, wondering how I was going to react to him, perhaps. 'You going to be around tomorrow?'

For a moment it crossed my mind that he was looking for someone to take Frederick back to London, but it turned out that Charlie had taken care of Frederick.

'Why?' I wanted to know.

'It's bloody embarrassing,' he began, and 'bloody embarrassing' was all he could find to say about having to go to court the next day to be charged with, among other things, unlawfully killing a child. And he wanted me to go with him to hold his hand.

At the time we were standing in one of those long, gloomy hospital corridors without any windows, lit by neon lights. After what Harvey had tried to do to Deirdre's son in an attempt to save his own skin, I never wanted to see him again. I wondered then that I had ever wanted to see him again after how he treated Deirdre, whom I already loved – I knew that now – all those years ago.

'I can't think why the hell I ever had anything to do with you in the first place,' I suddenly yelled at him. 'You've always been a shit – you were a shit at school, a shit at home, a shit in the army.'

People in white coats with stethoscopes round their necks or carrying ominous bowls and phials gave us a wide berth as they passed, glancing at us with raised eyebrows. Then, as a patient was pushed past on a squeaking trolley, someone with authority came up and firmly advised us gentlemen to continue our discussion outside.

I just looked at Harvey, who was standing there aghast and forlorn, turned on my heel and walked away. As I walked with my back to him down that seemingly endless corridor, I thought of him imitating owls, singing operatic arias, bowling overs, boasting about women, lying about business deals, importing pornography, lying to his children, lying to his wives, lying to his friends, lying about his friends, and I hoped that I would never see him again.

But of course I did.

I was told, because people always tell you things even if you would rather they didn't, when Harvey came out of prison. My first reaction was that it wouldn't affect me and that I had no need to think about it. I was busy at work and had plenty of other things on my mind without having to bother about Harvey. But I had no sooner decided to forget about him again than I found my thoughts returning to him with unpleasing frequency. I feared that he might try to get in touch despite the fact that my last communication had been anything but friendly, and I feared being drawn back once again into his life. Knowing Harvey, I supposed he would have conveniently expunged the details of our last meeting from his mind and, needing friends, he would surely turn to me, his oldest friend, regardless of the fact that I had made a point of not visiting him in prison. He would never be able to see that Deirdre and I would be better off without him.

As it turned out, I heard nothing from Harvey for over a year after he was released and, if it hadn't been for the fact that Moira, drunker than ever, lives in our street, I think I might really have begun to forget about him once and for all if one Sunday morning he had not decided to ring the front-door bell. I had just taken the paper and a cup of coffee to Deirdre in bed and was on my way back downstairs.

I opened the door, probably expecting a Jehovah's Witness, and there on the steps was Harvey.

Now I hadn't seen Harvey for five years or more. Not since I walked away from him in that hospital corridor.

'Jeremy Webber!' he said. 'Good to see you.'

I stared at him in amazement. He looked scruffy and shifty and didn't want to meet my eye. I didn't want to see him. I wanted him to go away.

'Harvey,' I said, feeling suddenly angry. 'You are not welcome in this house. I think you'd better just leave.'

Harvey began to wave his arms around in the old manner I knew so well. 'Let me come in for a moment,' he almost wailed. 'Jeremy, you're my oldest friend and I need help.'

Standing on the doorstep above him, I was for once taller than Harvey. 'I'm sorry,' I said, 'there is nothing I can do to help you.'

'Now you're being judgemental,' Harvey whinged.

Judgemental! Where the hell did Harvey, of all people, pick up jargon words like that? In prison, I supposed. Funny, I thought, the way people use that word as an ultimate judgement of someone else's behaviour when what they really mean is that they don't want that other person to think ill of them when they have done something they know to be bad.

'If you mean that I have a poor opinion of someone lying so that an innocent person takes the blame for a child's death, then, yes, I am.' I paused. 'Harvey, you must go, I'm sorry.'

'Come on, old boy,' Harvey said as he came up one step nearer the door. 'You know it wasn't quite like that. You do realize, don't you, that there was a miscarriage of justice? The police lied. They couldn't prove a thing about who was sitting where. I wasn't driving that car. Will and I changed places after we left the pub, halfway up the hill. But never mind. It's all over now – a thing of the past. Quite of the p-p-past. Shouldn't mention it really – not fair on the b-b-boy.' He glanced at the ground, avoiding my eye. Then he waved an arm half-heartedly in what seemed like a tired effort to revert to his old form. 'And now I've got this wonderful plan – import – export – you know the sort of thing. Only trouble is, I've had a few problems lately . . .'

I'll say.

'But you see, I know a man – a man I met in – well, never mind where I met him. Stanley. He's a good man, Stanley.'

I must have looked doubtful.

'A clever man. A very clever man. I'm thinking of doing business with him. It's an incredible opportunity – Central America – Colombia – Peru – Thailand. The only problem is, I need a bit of capital . . . I was wondering if . . .'

'Harvey,' I said, 'I am not lending you a farthing.' And so saying, I went inside and closed the front door behind me, but as I closed it, I had the fleeting, disquieting thought that Harvey might just for once have been telling the truth. Could there really have been a miscarriage of justice? Was Harvey's story ultimately the story of the boy who cried 'Wolf!'?

How could I ever be sure? All I knew was that I had to dispel that thought for ever from my mind or it would lie there like a canker waiting to spread until it poisoned my relationship with Will and then – God forbid – with Deirdre too.

I tried not to think about Harvey, but about six months after he came to the door, I bumped into Moira in the street outside. She gave me a bleary-eyed drunken look and I felt obliged to pause for a chat. She told me then that Harvey was back in prison.

It was after that, unable to put him quite out of my mind, that I decided to sit down to write Harvey's story. I thought long and hard about how to approach the subject. I thought about lies and betrayal and love, and I thought about Harvey endlessly trying to ingratiate himself through fantasy and fabrication so that at one moment I even began to feel sorry for him, because you can't lie and be loved. Thus Harvey has finally managed to alienate his whole family and even his oldest friends.

Sometimes I feel that I have been tainted by Harvey's lies which have run through my life like a vein of poison contaminating those of us who have been touched by them, and then I look back at the good times and remember that we were all genuinely attached to Harvey years ago. I remember the admiration and the envy I felt for him, yet now I do not feel that I can ever forgive him.

I wonder if any of the people who laughingly used to say that someone ought to write a book about Harvey ever really thought that when it was done, it would be done in a spirit of revenge.